Summer Term at
TREBIZON

Summer Term at TREBIZON

ANNE DIGBY

EGMONT

EGMONT

We bring stories to life

Summer Term at Trebizon
First edition published in Great Britain 1979 by W. H. Allen
This edition published 2016
by Egmont UK Limited
The Yellow Building, 1 Nicholas Road, London W11 4AN

ISBN 978 1 4052 8065 5

www.egmont.co.uk

A CIP catalogue record for this title is available from the British Library

62825/1

Typeset in Goudy Old Style by Avon DataSet Ltd, Bidford on Avon,
Warwickshire
Printed and bound in Great Britain by CPI Group

Stay safe online. Any website addresses listed in this book are correct
at the time of going to print. However, Egmont is not responsible
for content hosted by third parties.

Please be aware that online content can be subject to change and websites can
contain content that is unsuitable for children. We advise that all children are
supervised when using the internet.

CONTENTS

For Ella

ONE
A Maths Problem

For Rebecca Mason there were going to be a lot of good things about the summer term at Trebizon – and a few bad ones, too. The bad things all seemed to have a connection with the letter 'M'.

M stood for maths. It also stood for Maxwell. Worst of all, it stood for Mason, her own surname, and that was going to create its own problems.

Rebecca suspected none of this as the long distance bus trundled through the green English countryside. She had spent the Easter holidays at her grandmother's home in Gloucestershire, one of a group of 'retirement bungalows' on a small housing estate. She loved her gran but she had missed seeing London and her parents. The London house was let out until July, and her parents were in Saudi

Arabia. Her father had been posted there by his firm the previous September and Rebecca had been transferred from her local day school to Trebizon, a boarding school in the west country. She had been lonely there at first, until she had made some friends. Her two best friends were Tish Anderson and Sue Murdoch.

Now she was travelling back to Trebizon for the summer term, and although to her grandmother she had pretended to groan about going back to school, she was secretly quite looking forward to it.

As yet, the letter 'M' had no significance in her life. She couldn't have cared less what letter her surname began with. As for Mr Maxwell-beginning-with-M (who liked to be called Max), she had never even met him. So that left only maths.

She did spare a few brief thoughts to those, as well she might in view of the warning letter she had had from her father. The question of maths crossed her mind as, her luggage having been transferred from the coach at Trebizon Bus Station to a waiting taxi, she was being driven at speed out of the top end of town in the direction of school. Rebecca's thoughts lingered just long enough on the subject of maths to wish that they had never been invented, then quickly passed on.

There was Trebizon Bay! As the taxi passed the last of the hotels on the fringe of the town and turned into open country she could see the waters of the big, blue bay in the distance, across the fields. Although it was still only the end of April, there was a glorious sun this afternoon, dazzling on the sea, and the air was warm. Rebecca knew that they were allowed to swim in the sea during the summer term.

'I wonder if we'd be allowed to today, after tea?' she thought. She felt sticky after her long journey. 'I'd like that.' She wound down the window of the taxi halfway and stuck her head out, so that the rushing air blew her long fair hair around her face. Now she could just glimpse the school buildings in the parkland over on the west side of the bay, old roofs and white stone gables amongst tall trees that had recently burst into leaf. Trebizon School was still there then, as solid as ever.

Soon the taxi turned in through the main school gates, slowed down to ten m.p.h., as instructed, then dawdled along the long leafy lane that led to the main school building, which had once been a manor house. They passed one or two cars coming from the direction of the school, but most girls had arrived back in the early afternoon. The taxi-driver knew the ropes and crawled straight past old school and right round behind the dining hall block, eventually pulling up in the cobbled yard at the back of Juniper House: the long red-brick boarding house where all the junior girls at Trebizon, including Rebecca, lived. The driver opened the rear door of the taxi while Rebecca got out, arms laden with carrier bags and a tennis racket, the overspill from her trunk.

'Rebecca!' shrieked several voices at once.

'Tish!' laughed Rebecca. 'Sue! Mara –!'

They were all running towards her. In front was Ishbel Anderson, Tish for short, her dark curly hair badly in need of a comb. Behind her Sue Murdoch, Mara Leonodis and Margot Lawrence looked equally dishevelled. They had just finished a game of tennis and were carrying rackets. 'Elf' – chubby Sally Elphinstone – brought up the rear, carrying some tennis balls. She had been keeping score and was not sweaty and untidy like the others.

'About time you got here,' said Tish.

'It was that bus again,' said Rebecca. 'What a journey!'

'Where's this to, miss?' asked the taxi-driver. He was getting Rebecca's trunk out of the large boot.

'Upstairs?'

'Second floor!' interjected Sue promptly. 'Dormitory number six. We'll show you. You won't believe this but she's supposed to be unpacked by tea time!'

Sue led the way to the back door of Juniper House, followed by three of them, chattering. Tish hung back with Rebecca and the taxi man and yelled out:

'Catch, Margot!'

She hurled her tennis racket through the air as the black girl turned swiftly. Deftly Margot caught it.

'Now I can help you hump this trunk upstairs,' said Tish to the man.

With a great deal of awkwardness and laughter she did so, once colliding with Rebecca who was just behind them so that Rebecca dropped her things all over the stairs. Tish seemed to think that was hilarious. On the second floor landing they picked their way through the empty cases and trunks that were waiting to be collected and at last deposited the trunk safely inside dormitory six, at the foot of Rebecca's bed.

'Thanks!' said the taxi-driver to Tish. 'Your friend can get unpacked now.'

Rebecca dumped her other things on her bed and scrabbled around to find her purse. She paid the taxi-driver self-consciously, as she was not very used to hiring taxis, and just guessed wildly when it came to the tip, hoping it was neither too generous nor too mean.

'Thank you, miss,' he said, to Rebecca's relief. He thought she seemed a pretty youngster, athletic-looking, too. He glanced at the tennis racket on her bed and winked. 'You off to Wimbledon then?'

'Some hopes!' laughed Rebecca, blushing.

'Rebecca's going to be a sprinter!' said Tish.

'A sprinter, eh? You'll have your eye on the Olympics then.'

They all laughed, and as he left Elf called out:

'Someone in our form really has been to Wimbledon. Junior Wimbledon.'

'Hope she got a good seat,' he observed.

'No –' Elf started to follow him. 'She *played* there –'

'Now, now, Elf,' said Sue, hauling her back. 'He knows. Stop showing off about Joss. She wouldn't like it.'

'How is Joss?' asked Rebecca. 'Seen her yet?'

Josselyn Vining was head of games in the junior house, but had been away most of last term after a minor back operation.

'Fitter than ever!' said Sue. 'Saw her down on the courts –'

'Beating Miss Willis,' added Tish.

Rebecca sighed. It must be very satisfying to be like Joss Vining, brilliant at any game she turned her hand to and a natural leader. Or was it? It must set you just a little apart from everyone else.

All five girls rallied round to help Rebecca get

unpacked at speed, then dragged her empty trunk out on to the landing just as the first tea bell went. There were squeals then and a stampede into the washroom; hands and faces were washed and hair combed, Rebecca's included.

'Nice to see you back, Rebecca,' said Mara, waiting for her comb.

'Nice to *be* back,' confessed Rebecca.

Even better than being like Josselyn Vining, Rebecca decided, was being one of a crowd. Tish and Sue were her best friends because dramatic happenings in her first two terms had drawn them very close together. But the other three, Mara Leonodis, Margot Lawrence and Sally Elphinstone, were the sort Rebecca liked too. They all joined forces sometimes, especially when things needed doing – the 'Action Committee' Tish called it – and they certainly got things done. There were two other girls in the dormitory, both very pleasant, but it was these five she was with now that Rebecca liked best of all.

'I wonder if we'll need the Action Committee for anything this term?' said Rebecca, working furiously at a tangle.

'Only Charity Week,' said Mara.

'Charity Week?'

'Yes,' smiled Mara. 'And that'll be enough excitement for me.' There was a light in the Greek girl's eyes. 'This term I'm going to work very, very hard.'

'You *are*?' exclaimed Tish, with interest.

Mara had to burst out with it.

'If I work very hard, I may go into the A stream when we move up into the Third Year next term! It was in my report!'

'Oh, Mara!'

'Great!'

They all crowded round, patting Mara on the back. They were all Second Years at present and in the same form together, II Alpha, with the sole exception of Mara, who was in II Beta. She so much wanted to be in the same form as the rest of them. Now perhaps, when they moved up into III Alpha, Mara would be joining them!

'Anything wrong, Rebeck?' asked Tish, a moment later.

There was a funny look on Rebecca's face, for she had been reminded of something that she distinctly wanted to forget. But she quickly shook her head.

'Hey, listen!' said Sue, opening wide the

washroom door. 'It's the second bell. We're late!'

They all rushed down the west staircase, out of the front of Juniper House, which overlooked the quadrangle gardens and old school opposite, and along the terrace to the modern dining hall block. The doors were open and the clamour of noise hit Rebecca like a tidal wave. It sounded like four hundred girls talking at once which was, very roughly, the position.

The next day, Wednesday, when the term really started, they would have to sit at their proper tables. Today, girls could sit where they liked. The six latecomers had to take seats where they could find them and Rebecca found herself sitting with Mara and Sue at the same table as Roberta Jones, who had written a play in the Easter holidays.

'I shall be inviting people to be in it,' she said stolidly.

'But what's it for exactly, Roberta?' asked Rebecca.

'For Juniper's Charity Week of course,' said Roberta.

This being Rebecca's first summer at Trebizon,

Sue had to explain to her that early in May each year Juniper House organised a Charity Week. All the members of the junior boarding house, the entire First and Second Years, split up into small groups. Each group had to think of a fundraising idea and organise it, outside of lesson times, and then carry it out during the course of the week. 'It's quite fun,' Sue explained. 'There are different things going on every day.'

The girls in the group that raised the most money would get special merit marks from the Principal.

'I see what you mean about the Action Committee now!' said Rebecca, turning to Mara.

'That's a thought,' said Sue. 'We'd be good together. We'll get Tish to revive it, shall we?'

'Let's have a meeting and try and think of something really different,' said Rebecca, pushing her bowl forward for another helping of fruit salad and whipped cream. 'When?'

'I've got to go and do some music practice in a minute,' said Sue.

'I've got to check all my maths holiday work with my new calculator,' said the new, industrious Mara. 'Let's all be thinking of some ideas and talk about it tonight!'

'Right,' agreed Rebecca, but she felt suddenly depressed.

Maths!

Her father's letter came back to her mind with a jolt.

Your maths are letting you down, Becky. You must try very hard next term.

Enclosed with the letter had been a photocopy of her school report, which had been sent out to her parents. On the whole it had been good, but beside *Mathematics* Miss Gates had written: *Generally poor. Some improvement this term but Rebecca has a great deal of ground to make up.*

However, it wasn't that which had filled her with alarm. It was the Principal's comment, right at the bottom of the report:

Rebecca has high ability in some subjects, but unless she makes noticeable progress in maths next term it may be advisable for her to spend the next academic year in the Beta stream, where she can receive extra maths teaching.
(Signed) Madeleine Welbeck. Principal.

So, just as Mara was excited at the possibility of

going up next year, Rebecca was dismayed at the possibility of going down. No wonder Tish had noticed a funny look on her face. Now Sue noticed something, too.

'Anything wrong?'

'Tell you later.'

Rebecca decided she would tell both Sue and Tish about it, straight after tea. That's what best friends were for. They would find some way of cheering her up.

She was right about that.

TWO
Learning to Surf

Tea was over. Rebecca and Sue waited outside the dining hall, on the terrace, for Tish. Through the glass doors they could see that she was talking to Zrina Singh, one of the prefects on duty. When she was happy, Tish Anderson had the biggest grin in the whole school and it was very much in evidence as she charged through the door to join them.

'Still feel like going in the sea, Rebecca?'

'*Yes!*' Rebecca had mentioned swimming to Tish, almost as soon as she'd got out of the taxi. 'Why? Can we?'

'Anybody who's got their swimming certificate can! Zrina says we've got to wait for our tea to go down, but there's plenty of time because Harry's on duty till half-past seven. He's the lifeguard.'

Rebecca felt excited. She was a good swimmer and had gained her swimming certificate during the winter term. There was an indoor pool in the school sports centre. But she had yet to swim in Trebizon Bay. She hadn't really thought they would be allowed to yet! In spite of the warm, sunny day, the sea was bound to be cold until the summer got under way.

'We won't want to swim, of course,' said Tish surprisingly. 'Too cold.'

'We won't?' asked Rebecca, baffled. 'Then –'

'Surfing!' said Tish. 'In wetsuits! The school's got all its own stuff, in that white shed next to our beach huts. Harry looks after it for us. Ever done it?'

'No –' Surfing!

'Wait till you try. Harry'll show you!'

'Blow,' said Sue. 'I've got music practice.'

The three of them walked along the terrace and into Juniper House and then they went up to the dormitory. Sue changed out of her tennis things and into her school skirt and blue striped summer blouse. It had a V neck and short sleeves; the girls didn't have to wear a tie in the summer term. To the lapel she pinned the pretty little badge with the monogram HC that showed that she was now one

15

of the school's Music Scholars. As Tish and Sue chattered about the Juniper House Charity Week and the need to get the Action Committee going again, Rebecca fell silent.

'Terrific!' said Tish. 'Let's try and think of a really good fundraising idea tonight. Let's try and be the winning group.'

Sue picked up her violin case. It was time for her to go over to the Hilary Camberwell Music School, but she glanced at Rebecca.

'Come on, Rebecca. Out with it.'

Rebecca had been just waiting for the chance to tell them about her maths problem. Now she did, gloomily.

She wasn't gloomy for very long.

'What rubbish!' exclaimed Tish. 'So that's what you've been brooding about! They won't put you in the B stream next year! You're good at everything else and you just need to catch up on maths, that's all.'

'It's just to get you working, Rebecca,' said Sue. 'They threaten you! They did exactly the same thing to me last year – said I'd go into II Beta if I wasn't careful. I was miles behind the others because we had a crazy kind of maths teacher at my last school, and I never knew what Miss Gates was talking about half the time –'

'That's just it!' said Rebecca with feeling. 'And I don't this year. All the maths was different at my day school and the trouble with Gatesy is she takes it for granted that we know all the back work. Well, I *don't*. So how am I ever going to catch up?'

'Because we have Mrs Shaw this term!' explained Sue, in triumph.

'That's what saved Sue's bacon last year,' said Tish.

'Mrs Shaw?'

'Yes,' said Tish. 'You haven't met her yet. She comes in every summer term to teach the juniors because Gatesy gets all tied up with the seniors and their big exams.'

'The nice thing about Mrs Shaw,' explained Sue, 'is that instead of taking it for granted that everyone's brilliant she takes it for granted that everyone's as thick as two short planks. She explains things over and over again!'

'Phew!' Rebecca laughed. She was overcome by a feeling of utmost relief. 'Mrs Shaw.' She repeated the name, with gratitude. What a friendly comforting name it began to seem. Shaw. Sure. Safe. 'Just the person I need!'

'Just the person we all need, seeing there's exams at the end of term,' said Sue. She moved away from the other two. 'I'd better get along to the Hilary. Everything'll be all right, Rebecca, you'll see.'

'Bound to be,' said Tish. 'Hey, Margot!' As Sue went out of the dormitory, Margot Lawrence came in. 'We can surf! Coming? Help teach Rebecca!'

A quarter of an hour later, the three of them strolled through the leafy little wood at the back of Juniper House and came out through a private gate into Trebizon Bay. There was still some sun. They had been trying to think of a fundraising idea for Charity Week, without success, and now all they could think about was surfing. They could change into wetsuits in the school beach huts. They had brought towels to dry themselves with, after they came out of the sea, and jumpers in case they felt cold later on.

They clambered through the dunes and out on to the open expanse of sand. Rebecca was beginning to feel very happy, looking around her as they walked across the sand to the white shed by the beach huts, where the lifeguard kept the school wetsuits and Malibu boards.

'Just look at that man!' exclaimed Rebecca. 'Isn't he good!'

A sinewy young man, with MAX in white letters across the chest of his wetsuit, was riding in on the surf from a long way out. He stood balanced sideways on his Malibu board, legs apart, coming in at great speed, the spray kicking up in front of him – at the same time managing to wave to his girlfriend who was watching him admiringly from the shore.

All the other surfers were Trebizon girls, about a dozen of them. It was a huge bay, the sand hard and golden down near the sea. The waves broke far out and came rolling in, in a long and seemingly unbroken line, to make it a surfers' paradise. In this corner of the bay, where the girls were allowed to surf this evening, the waves were breaking closer in to shore, making the run-ins shorter, but very exciting nevertheless. Here, Harry was able to keep a watchful eye on them all. The school's white Malibu boards lay in a row on the sand, their fins uppermost, looking like a row of sleeping sharks.

When Rebecca had changed into a wetsuit he selected her a board and took her in hand, wading into the shallows with her. He was a tough, weatherbeaten man whose skin looked almost as dark as Margot's against his faded blue denim swimming shorts and white tee shirt. First Rebecca tried riding in on the edge of the waves, flat on her stomach, hands gripping the two edges of the hollow fibreglass board, and that was easy. Then she tried to stand up on the board in the eddying, swirling shallows, with plenty of encouragement from Tish and Margot, until they went off to do some real surfing.

After a few minutes, Rebecca was keeping her balance well and longed to get out of the shallows. The fin at the back of the board kept scraping into the sand and bringing her to a halt. She could see the others surfing. Tish was good, so was Margot. They could do it!

'Come on, Rebecca!'

'Shall I?' she asked Harry eagerly. He nodded.

'Go and have a try. You have to get out to beyond the breakers.'

Rebecca lay flat on the board, as she had seen the others do, then propelled it forward by paddling with her hands to get beyond the breaker line. She enjoyed rising up through the big waves and feeling the sting of the spray on her cheeks and the salty tang of the sea on her lips. The sun was getting low in the west now, blood red, turning to pink some little clouds on the horizon. She kept going until she was out beyond the breakers and level with Tish.

'Get the board like this,' Tish shouted, and demonstrated, 'and when a big one comes – just get on, and go!'

Rebecca waited for the next big breaker.

As it came, she sprang on to the board in front of it and then felt herself being lifted high into the air. Then she started to shoot forward at speed.

'Fantastic!' she shrieked. She wobbled from crouching to standing position, sideways on. 'I'm standing up!' she cried in disbelief. 'I'm actually –'

She wobbled perilously on the Malibu board, struggling to keep her balance as it raced along in front of the surging breaker. The shore was rushing towards her. She could see Harry waving. She tried to change position.

'Ohhh!'

Rebecca lost her balance and went keeling into the sea with a great splash. The big wave went right over her head. After a few moments she bobbed up on to the surface of the sea, laughing and gasping for breath, her eyes screwed up tight and full of salt water.

She opened them and started to thrash around to get a grip on her Malibu board. She never even saw the fast approaching surfer. He was going extremely gracefully and he didn't want to spoil it.

'Look out!' he yelled.

Even as Rebecca was still blinking the water out of her eyes and wondering from which direction the voice was coming, he went straight over her board in a somersault and took a nose dive into the sea. When he came up he was gulping for air and looking cross.

He swam to get his own red surfboard, painted to look like a fish. Bobbing on the sea, fin uppermost, it looked quite alarming.

He started to laugh. He was really very good looking.

'Are you all right, darling?' called his girlfriend from the beach. He turned his back on Rebecca and kickpaddled himself and his board towards the shore. Rebecca followed, slowly. She heard him call out.

'I'm fine, Katie. Some of these girls aren't very bright! How about a drink now?'

That was Rebecca's very first meeting with Max.

A minute later, Harry blew a long blast on the whistle and it was time for them all to come out of the sea.

THREE
Roberta Falls in Love

'Well, what did you think of it?' asked Tish.

'Need you ask!' exclaimed Rebecca.

The three of them were warmly dressed now, walking back along the beach to school. Harry was locking all the equipment away in the white shed, ready for another day. Rebecca's cheeks were aglow.

'You certainly look cheerful!' said Margot. 'Even if you did come off!'

'Right in front of that man!' giggled Tish.

'When can we come again?' asked Rebecca, rapturously. 'Now I've tried it I really want to get good at it, like you two. What a sensation! Did you know –' she said suddenly, 'that in 1936 a man rode a wave a distance of 4,500 feet?'

'Oh, Rebecca!' laughed Margot. 'Where?'

24

'Off the coast of Hawaii,' said Rebecca solemnly. She had a mind that hoarded useless snippets of information. Each week she wrote a little piece called 'Did You Know?' for *The Juniper Journal*, a newsletter that the juniors produced themselves. She never seemed to run out of facts for it.

'4,500 feet!' said Tish. 'Lucky for him you weren't around then, or you might have spoiled the whole thing.' They all started to smile. 'Just imagine –' Tish threw her arms wide '– all set to break the world record, the crowds cheering, the flags waving and then suddenly, up pops Rebecca, looking for her Malibu board . . . !'

'Ooops – crash! – sorry!' laughed Rebecca.

They had just reached the sand dunes. Margot suddenly thought of something. She turned and looked at the bay, beautiful and empty now. The sea was reddening in the setting sun and the long line of white breakers had never looked more racy.

'Got it!' she exclaimed. 'Stop a minute, you two.'

'Got what?' they asked, stopping.

'Record-breakers! Raising money. Charity Week!' said Margot.

'Surfing!' yelled Tish. 'Yes, you *have* got it –'

'Maybe one of us could try and set some kind of

record –' began Margot.

'What, a long-distance record?' asked Rebecca, in disbelief.

'No, no,' said Tish. 'Wait, I'm thinking.' She stared at the distant breakers and then clapped her hands. 'Just the number of trips! The number of times we can come in from beyond the breakers to the shore, without falling off. If you come off, you're out!'

'And we can each get sponsors!' said Margot eagerly. 'People have to promise to pay a penny for each ride we make –'

'Or even two pence,' said Tish in delight. 'The rich ones.'

'That's really good,' admitted Rebecca. 'Sponsored surfing. Bet no one else will think of it! Oh, I wish I could go in for it!'

'Maybe you can!' said Tish. 'You've got a couple of weeks to learn!'

'What about the others?' asked Rebecca, meaning the rest of the Action Committee.

'Couldn't be better,' said Margot. 'Sue's good and so's Elf. Mara, well –'

'Mara hates surfing,' realised Tish. 'But she can be in charge. Somebody's got to be. Somebody's got to have a chart and tick off each time we ride in without falling off. Come on! Let's find them and see what they think!'

They turned their eyes away from the sea and ran back to school.

They found Mara Leonodis and Sally Elphinstone straight away. They were leaning against a radiator in the corridor outside the Second Year Common Room gossiping.

'Action Committee all ready?' asked Mara.

'Let's go in and find some armchairs!' suggested Tish. 'We'll tell you what we've thought of. Besides, we've been surfing and our legs are aching.'

'No fear!' said Elf. 'Roberta's in there, jabbering about her play for Charity Week. She's had loads of copies typed out in the holidays –'

'She'll put one into your hand the minute you walk in,' warned Mara. 'Apparently it needs a cast of at least twenty people!'

'We've thought of our own thing to do!' said Tish. 'At least, Margot has. Here, let's go in the kitchen.'

'Sue!' said Rebecca as she opened the door of the kitchen. Sue was munching sandwiches. 'Who you hiding from?'

'Who d'you think?' mumbled Sue.

'Don't you *want* to be in A *Midsummer Night's Nightmare* then?' asked Tish. 'Hey! Where did you get those sandwiches?'

'Left over from the train – here, have some.'

The three girls who had been surfing grabbed at the food eagerly: Rebecca was amazed to  find herself so hungry again. She had eaten a big tea. Between delicious mouthfuls of bread and butter and cream cheese they expounded the 'sponsored surfing' plan. It was an immediate hit.

'Perfect!' said Sue. Then, gazing at the empty place where her sandwiches had been: 'And afterwards we'd better have some sponsored sandwich cutting, at the rate you three can eat.'

Elf laughed. She felt quite excited. She was terrible at organised games but she enjoyed swimming and surfing and was quite good at both. This was due – the others said – to her being more buoyant than average.

'What about you, Mara?' Tish asked anxiously.

'Fine!' smiled Mara, who liked Tish very much

and would always follow her lead. 'Like you say, I can keep count, and help collect the money up afterwards and all that sort of thing.'

'We could raise pounds!' said Rebecca eagerly. Secretly she was determined to get good at surfing in time for Charity Week, and intended to practise whenever she possibly could. She wanted to take part and at least do a few rides without falling off!

'It's all settled then,' said Tish. She gazed round at the group and said humorously: 'I hereby declare the Action Committee re-awakened!'

There was a happy hum of conversation as they moved around the kitchen making cocoa and finding biscuits. There would be quite a lot of things to do. They would have to get permission, naturally, and Miss Morgan – their House Mistress – would want to make sure that the surfing was all properly supervised. Then they would need to make sponsorship forms. Tish could type those out on a stencil and run them off on the little duplicator that Mara's father had given to the junior boarding house, the machine they used when printing *The Juniper Journal*.

After a while, Rebecca heard voices in the corridor and peeped out of the kitchen door, her cocoa in her hand. Roberta Jones was leaving the Second Year Common Room at last, accompanied by Debbie Rickard and the Nathan twins. They were all holding copies of the play.

'I expect everyone will want to be in it,' Debbie was saying. 'How will you choose?'

'I shall hold auditions if that happens,' said Roberta.

'Coast is clear!' said Rebecca, when they'd gone. 'Now we can go and drink our cocoa in there.'

They trooped into the big, comfortable Common Room with its armchairs and rugs and big windows. It was up on the first floor of Juniper House. Through the windows Rebecca could see the school's formal gardens, set within the quadrangle of buildings, shadowy and peaceful in the dusk. Here and there a lighted window in the old school opposite illuminated a rose bush, a flagstone or a triangle of lawn.

'It's nearly dark,' said Sue, switching on the lights.

Over by a window, Jenny Brook-Hayes got up from her chair, put down her book and started to draw the long curtains.

'Look, Robert's put a notice up,' said Tish.

They crowded round the big noticeboard behind the door. The notice said:

IMPORTANT CHARITY WEEK
The Fairy Queen by Roberta Jones
The first reading of my one-act play will take place in here, Friday dinner hour. Everyone who wants a part please sign below and then come along to the play-reading. Make this play a success and be one of the group that raises the most funds for Charity Week.

(Signed) R. Jones

'Nobody's signed yet,' observed Rebecca. 'What's it like?' she asked, wandering across to Jenny, who had settled back with her novel.

'Not much good,' Jenny grunted, still reading.

'I don't mean your book, I mean the play,' said Rebecca.

'So do I,' said Jenny. She looked up and sighed. 'She's actually hoping we might pass it forward to be considered for *The Trebizon*, too.'

'Not again,' groaned someone. Every term Roberta Jones tried to get something on the shortlist for *The Trebizon Journal*, the school's official magazine. At

31

present Jenny was the Magazine Officer for Juniper House and decided which junior contributions should go on the shortlist. A vote was taken on the shortlist and the best ones submitted. They usually then appeared in the magazine, a great honour.

'Hope people will find time to do some good things,' said Jenny suddenly. 'I mean, with Charity Week coming up. This'll be Audrey's last term and she'll want it to be her best issue.'

Audrey Maxwell, the Editor of *The Trebizon Journal*, was in the Upper Sixth and would be going up to University in the autumn.

'Oh, they'll find time,' said Rebecca. People always clamoured to get in *The Trebizon*. Rebecca herself wouldn't be trying this term, having already had two pieces of writing published – the first in very unusual circumstances, in her first term. But there were plenty of others who were dying to get into print. She settled on the arm of Jenny's chair. 'So you're not thinking of being in the play?'

'Joanna and Joss and I have decided to run a cake stall.'

'We're doing something else, too,' said Sue, coming up and joining them. 'Just thought of it this evening.'

Rebecca sighed and sipped her cocoa. The sponsored surfing was going to be marvellous, but she felt a twinge of sympathy for Roberta. She was large and not very pretty and always rather full of herself. She had the idea that she was a great writer,

although she was actually much better at other things, like netball and hockey. She was quite good at lessons, too, except for maths – like Rebecca. But she had this terrible urge to write things and show people how good they were all the time. Would anybody even want to be in *The Fairy Queen* except the Nathan twins, who were loyal friends of Roberta's, and maybe Debbie Rickard?

Rebecca was feeling sleepier and sleepier and the hum of conversation in the Common Room was getting blurred. When Miss Morgan put her head round the door and said 'Bedtime!' she roused herself and went straight up to the dormitory, without even waiting for the others. It had been a long day.

'Hello, Rebecca, good holidays?' asked a slim, pretty girl as the Second Years filed into the assembly hall next morning.

'Yes thanks, Pippa!' said Rebecca shyly.

Pippa Fellowes-Walker was in the Lower Sixth and was already a prefect: Rebecca's favourite one. Rebecca was an only child and if she could have had an older sister, she would have wanted her to be like Pippa.

As the big hall filled up, Mr Barrington, the school's Director of Music, played the grand piano and the girls shuffled and chattered and scraped chairs as they got into their proper places. It was another warm day and the whole school wore summer uniform, open-necked striped blouses crisp and clean, blue skirts spotless, a few blue jumpers here and there for those who felt the cold. Silence fell as the Principal arrived to take Assembly, walking the hall in easy strides and mounting the stage.

'Good morning, girls.'

'Good morning, Miss Welbeck.'

As it was the first morning of term there were a lot of notices to give out and Rebecca still felt sleepy. She went off into a daydream. She came to just in time to hear Miss Welbeck finishing off an announcement:

'. . . So although we are sorry that Mrs Shaw,

who as you know comes here as a relief teacher every summer term, cannot be with us this year, we are indeed lucky to have procured his services at such short notice. He holds a First Class Honours degree in mathematics.'

Although a lot of the younger girls were bored and fidgety by this stage, and some of them looked half asleep, Rebecca was suddenly wide awake. Mrs Shaw not coming! A man coming in her place! A First Class Honours graduate – a high-powered mind – brilliant, wise, erudite. Rebecca's shoulders sagged.

'He'll probably be even worse than Miss Gates,' she said to Tish gloomily as they all trooped across to the form room in old building, after Assembly. 'Fancy someone like that needing a job, anyway.'

'Some old chap they've dragged out of retirement, I expect,' said Tish.

Sue glanced at Rebecca sympathetically.

'Cheer up. One thing about men teachers is they usually take pity on you more than women. They usually help you more. I mean, look at Mr Douglas.'

That raised Rebecca's spirits. It was true, their chemistry master was very kind and avuncular. At her London comprehensive school, too, there had been a lot of men teachers and on the whole she had got on very well with them.

'I'd still rather have Mrs Shaw,' said a voice behind them. It belonged to Roberta Jones. Her plaits, which never suited her at the best of times, looked particularly droopy this morning. 'She helped me a lot last summer. I don't like men teaching you, they never take any notice of you.'

'You ought to make yourself look glamorous, Robert,' said Tish with a giggle. 'Wear your hair loose and all that.'

Roberta scowled. 'Shut up!' She was in no mood for Ishbel Anderson's funny remarks. The truth, although she was not going to admit it to a soul, was that she was worried. She had received a report very similar to Rebecca's and her parents were going to be annoyed if she had to go into the B stream next year. She had to do well at maths this term!

A new teacher was always interesting. The eighteen girls in Rebecca's form could hardly wait for maths, which was second lesson on a Wednesday. No sooner had Miss Heath, their form-mistress, gone out of the room after taking them for English, than Tish and some others rushed for the door. The II Alpha form room was right at the top of the old manor house and with luck if they hung over the banisters they might catch a glimpse of the new master coming up the stairs.

Rebecca and Sue, who shared a desk at the back, remained seated however, getting their maths things ready. Rebecca felt slightly anxious.

'I thought all my problems were over when you told me about Mrs Shaw!' she said. 'Now I don't know.'

'Don't worry, Rebecca.' Sue nudged her arm. 'He'll probably be all right. And even if he isn't, they just threaten you in school reports. They don't mean it.'

There was a lot of din outside, like a stampede. The door burst open and the girls came rushing back in to their desks, shouting and laughing.

'He's coming!'

'You should see him!'

'What's he like, Tish?' asked Rebecca, as Tish scrambled into her chair and rummaged around in her desk for her maths things. Tish looked across the gangway at Sue and Rebecca and her eyes were sparkling with fun. 'He's young! Dark hair. Looks like –'

'Ssssshhh!'

The new maths master walked in, tall and sinewy and very good looking, with dark curly hair. Rebecca recognised him at once. It was the brilliant surfer who had been down in Trebizon Bay.

'Hello,' he said, with an engaging smile. He went and sat on the edge of the table in front of the blackboard and surveyed the girls. They surveyed him back. 'I'm Mr Maxwell. My friends call me Max. You can, too.'

The girls of Form II Alpha grinned and whispered and nudged each other, hardly able to believe their luck. Not only did Mr Maxwell – Max – look dishy but he seemed easy-going, too. Rebecca, on the other hand, felt rather disconcerted – especially as, only last night, she had sent the new maths master toppling into the sea. She hoped he wouldn't hold it against her.

Meanwhile Roberta Jones was staring at him. She shared a desk in the front row with Aba Amori, the Nigerian girl, just next to her friends, the Nathan twins. So she had a really good view of the new master. Her rather red, stolid face was getting redder and redder with pleasure and self-importance.

'Haven't I met you somewhere before?' she blurted out.

Max looked at her from under his long, dark lashes, hesitated for a moment, then gave her a flashing smile.

'My girlfriend says I look like an actor.'

Everyone giggled.

'But I have!' protested Roberta, frowning hard in concentration, trying to remember. She wasn't going to have her moment of importance snatched away from her. 'I'm trying to think –'

Max stood up, picked up a piece of chalk and walked to the blackboard, firmly turning his back on Roberta. He began to write.

'Right. Let's start today by refreshing our minds on the binary and denary systems . . .'

'I remember!' Roberta shouted. 'You were at Greencourt!'

The master's hand stopped in the middle of chalking up some numbers. His back view remained frozen for a moment then, slowly, he lowered his arm, turned round, and walked over to Roberta. Her face was upturned, as she gazed at him.

'You never taught me but you used to teach the top class. I remember! You weren't there very long, but I remember you!'

'And you are –?'

'Roberta Jones!' she said eagerly.

'Of course!' He looked down at her upturned face and smiled. 'Little Bobbie Jones! Of course I remember you now. I did teach at your Prep School for a while – a term or two, wasn't it? – and, my, how you have grown! Well, isn't it a small world.'

'Yes,' breathed Roberta, almost speechless with pleasure.

'Ahem!' coughed Tish and there was some suppressed giggling.

'Well, to work,' said Max brightly, striding to the blackboard, but looking back over his shoulder to give Roberta a friendly nod. 'I'm sure Bobbie will make quick work of this exercise. How about the rest of you?'

Roberta watched, transfixed, as he wrote the numbers up on the board.

'Robert's fallen in love,' whispered Sue across the gangway to Tish.

'What a hoot!' grinned Tish.

Rebecca smiled rather weakly. Roberta was having some luck for once. How was she going to get on with the new master? Would he remember her from last night?

What were the binary and denary systems anyway?

FOUR
Two Views on Max

Rebecca watched the rows of figures appearing on the blackboard.

1011 . . . What on earth were they meant to represent?

'Start copying them down in your exercise books,' Max said, as the chalk squeaked across the board: 10011, 100111 . . . The rows seemed to be getting longer all the time! There was some bustle and the sound of flicking pages as the girls got their books open and started to write. Rebecca copied the numbers down from the blackboard as carefully as she could, at the same time whispering to Sue:

'What are they?'

'Binary numbers!' hissed Sue, as though that explained everything.

'Be quiet!' said Max, squatting to finish off the column of figures, which almost ran off the bottom of the blackboard. He got up, turned round, placed the chalk on his table and dusted his hands off. Then he lolled against the wall beside the blackboard, waiting for them to finish writing. Once or twice his gaze strayed to Roberta, and he seemed to be deep in thought.

'Right.' He came out of his reverie. A lot of the girls had put their ballpoint pens down and were gazing at him expectantly. 'Let me explain. I'm not going to do any new work with you this term. We're just going to go through everything step by step, that you've learnt in your first two years here. We're going to consolidate. Come the exams and you'll be tested on the whole lot. If you don't know it all by then, heaven help you. Anyone who gets less than fifty per cent in the maths exam, or bad marks in term time, or both, will go into the Beta stream next year! Or the Gamma stream! You're supposed to be the clever lot in this room.'

There was some slightly excited laughter. Max was

acting. They rather liked it. One or two rewarded his performance with long, realistic groans.

'Now, somebody tell me what these numbers are –' He pointed to Tish. 'You at the back with the curly hair. Name?'

'Ishbel Anderson.'

'Tish!' shouted several voices at once.

'Right, Tish. You tell me. What are they called and what will you do with them?'

'Binary numbers,' said Tish, happily. She had already decided that Max's lessons were going to be an improvement on those that Miss Gates dished out. 'And we're going to put them into denary numbers.'

'Precisely! Our minds are meeting!' said Max, giving her a dazzling smile. He then gazed round the room. 'You are to take each binary number in turn, work out its denary equivalent and write it alongside. Any girl not able to perform this simple task, put her hand up.' He waited.

All over the room, heads were quickly lowered over maths exercise books and girls began writing. Just two hands were raised. One was Roberta's and the other was Rebecca's.

'Please, Max,' said Roberta, 'it's over a year since

we did this and I just can't quite remember.'

'Okay, Bobbie,' he spoke soothingly. 'Come and sit beside me and we'll talk. It'll soon come back to you.'

'Thanks!' Roberta said, adding hastily: 'I just need to brush up – I know how to do it really.'

Max was staring fixedly at Rebecca.

'You are –?'

'Rebecca Mason.'

She knew at once that he had recognised her.

'Didn't I bump into you last night?' he said wittily.

'That's right,' said Rebecca. 'I fell off my Malibu board – I'm sorry.'

There were a few snorts.

'What's the problem now?'

'The problem is that I've never done it before.'

'Surfing?' asked Max and the whole class burst out laughing.

'No, I mean –' Rebecca began, her colour rising, 'I was at a different school last year and –'

'All right.' Max hardly seemed to be listening. 'I'll deal with Roberta first as she's only got a minor problem and then I'll get round to you.'

'Max thinks I'm dumb, I can tell,' thought

Rebecca.

Roberta had already scuttled up to his table. He drew up a spare chair and they sat there together, talking very quietly. Sue and Tish made some wildly comic faces at each other and at Rebecca and then bent over their work. Rebecca idly doodled a picture of a Malibu board with shark's teeth and waited for Max to finish with Roberta. She waited a long time. 'She's only supposed to have a minor problem!' thought Rebecca as she watched. Max kept scribbling numbers down on a notepad and explaining them in a low patient voice. As soon as he finished, Roberta would pipe up again with another question. Rebecca began to wonder if it might take the whole lesson.

Tish passed Rebecca a note, straight across Sue.

How long does it take when she's got a MAJOR problem? T.

They both hiccupped with laughter. Rebecca showed Sue the note and she laughed, too. 'Shut up!' requested Max. He continued to speak to Roberta and Rebecca continued to doodle on the cover of her book until, at long last, she heard the scraping of a chair up at the front of the class. Roberta returned to her desk, a self-satisfied smile on her face. She looked – Tish said later – as though she had just cracked Einstein's theory of relativity, single-handed.

With a sigh of relief, Rebecca waited to be summoned. Max sat behind his table sideways on, his long legs elegantly crossed, frowning in concentration. He seemed to be making some workings-out on his notepad. Rebecca gained the impression that he had completely forgotten her existence. Finally, too shy to call out, she scraped her chair back and started to get to her feet. Even as she did so, the door opened and Mrs Devenshire, the school secretary, appeared. She was out of breath and slightly cross at having to climb so many stairs. Her office was at the bottom of old school and the II Alpha form room, with its sloping ceilings and funny little windows, was right up at the top.

'You're wanted on the telephone, Mr Maxwell,' she said.

'Am I?' He beamed and sprang up and headed for the door, then stopped as he remembered his class. He turned to them. 'Work on. I'll be taking your books in at the end of the lesson and the marks will be going down on your weekly mark sheet. If any girl hasn't managed to finish I'll want to know what she's been doing – oh,' he realised for the first time that Rebecca was standing up. 'Look on my table and you'll find your last year's text book. Chapter Five I think it is. It'll refresh your memory.'

'I was at a different school last year –' Rebecca began again.

He shot out of the doorway. Rebecca walked up to his table and noticed that he'd been making a diagram on his notepad. It looked like a hang-glider, with a lot of measurements and calculations jotted all round it. She found a First Year maths text book, took it back and turned to Chapter Five.

'I think he's designing a hang-glider,' she whispered to Sue.

'Really?' said Sue.

'Hang-glider?' exclaimed Tish. 'Must have a look in a minute.' She bent her head over her work, going steadily through the numbers.

'Isn't he athletic looking?' said Judy Sharp, who sat the other side of Tish. 'Was he out surfing last night then?'

'Yes. And he's really good. Rebecca got in his way!'

'I bet hang-gliding's fun.' That was Josselyn Vining's voice, from further along the back row. 'I'd love to try it.' Trust Joss!

Soon, there was so much chattering and whispering going on at the back of the form room that Rebecca couldn't take in a word of Chapter Five. She envied the ease with which the others could do the work and discuss Max at the same time! She must find out about these wretched numbers!

'Sue!' she pleaded, as soon as Sue had put her pen down. 'Help me!'

'It's easy,' said Sue, pointing to the first row of figures. 'See that 1? Well it's not a 1 really, it's a 2. Get it?'

Rebecca didn't. Now there was a fresh diversion.

Tish had gone up to the front of the room and had found Max's design and was showing it round the class. Then she put it back and perched on the edge of the table. She swung her legs and surveyed everyone, just as Max had done when he first arrived.

'Hallo,' she declaimed, giving a horrible sickly grin and imitating Miss Gates's voice. 'My name's Miss Gates. My friends call me Gatesy. You can, too.'

Everyone hooted with laughter, even Debbie Rickard, who usually hated Tish. Roberta Jones

49

actually smiled and her eyes sparkled a little. Tish carried on in this vein, getting wilder and wilder, finally climbing up on to the table and flapping her arms up and down. 'Don't mind me, girls, but I'm just going off to do a little hang-gliding.'

The girls were almost in hysterics and Rebecca could feel the tears of mirth running down her cheeks. Crash! Tish leapt high into the air from the table, flapping her arms, and landed almost at the door.

'Bye, bye, girls!'

The door burst open. Tish found herself face to face with none other than Miss Gates herself, who had been just passing by. Tish's arms were still upraised. Slowly, very slowly, she lowered them to her sides. Slowly, too, the uproar in the form room subsided until it was no more than a few sniffs and snorts.

'Go to your desk, Ishbel,' said the grey-haired senior mistress. 'Who is taking this class?'

'I am,' said Max, sauntering in. 'What a racket!'

'I see you left them unattended,' commented Miss Gates icily.

'I'm sure they've all finished the work I set them,' said Max, quite unperturbed. 'Have you, girls?'

'Yes!' they all roared, anxious to protect Max from Miss Gates.

The bell for morning break sounded.

Miss Gates marched out of the room. As she went, Max gave her back view a solemn salute. It was all the girls could do to hold in their laughter. He then faced the class and clapped his hands.

'Books in, please.'

The eighteen members of Form II Alpha filed up with their maths exercise books and placed them in a pile. Roberta had hers open and showed it to Max. There was a very happy smile on her face.

'Done the whole lot, eh, Bobbie?' he said, abstractedly. 'Good for you.'

'I haven't done any at all,' said Rebecca apologetically, holding the text book. 'I'm afraid I still don't understand them.'

'Keep the book and learn Chapter Five off by heart,' he said briefly. 'It's all explained in words of one syllable. I'll test you tomorrow, if there's time.'

'It's not fair!' exclaimed Rebecca later, as she and Tish and Sue collected their orange squash and biscuits in the dining hall. 'He spends all that time with Roberta, who's done it before.'

'Robert's hopeless at maths,' interrupted Tish.

'– and then when it comes to me, he tells me to read it all up in a book. Now I've got some extra prep to do!'

'It hasn't really dawned on him yet that you weren't here last year,' said Sue. 'But he would have shown you, if his girlfriend hadn't rung him up in the middle of the lesson!'

They all laughed, but Rebecca said wryly:

'If I'd twisted his arm, he would. He thinks I'm useless, I can tell.'

At that moment Roberta walked into the dining

hall with the Nathan twins. She looked like someone in a happy daze.

'Robert's still glowing from it all!' said Tish. 'She can't believe her luck.'

'Glowing? Undoubtedly the Max factor,' cracked Sue. Tish and Rebecca groaned.

'What's Roberta got that I haven't?' inquired Rebecca, later. 'Whatever it is, I must try and cultivate it.'

'You'll be all right, Becky, don't worry,' said Tish, as they drank their squash. 'You heard what he said – he's going to go through everything we've done, step by step. You'll soon catch up. And you must admit it's going to be a lot of fun having him.'

'I suppose so,' nodded Rebecca. 'Though I'd like to have seen this Mrs Shaw. The one you said was so good.'

'Maybe,' conceded Sue. 'But I'll tell you something –' she pushed her spectacles up her nose and grinned, 'Max is better looking than Mrs Shaw.'

'*And* Miss Gates,' said Tish. 'Put together.'

'Especially put together, I should think,' said Rebecca.

They laughed.

* * *

Evelyn Gates spent the morning break with Madeleine Welbeck, the Principal of Trebizon. They had been drinking coffee together in Miss Welbeck's panelled study in the school's main building, once an eighteenth-century manor house. The study's first floor windows overlooked ancient parkland. The huge oaks had lost their bare brown winter outlines and were dense with young green leaves. The morning sun slanted amongst them on to rolling hillocks of grass and Miss Welbeck, half-closing her eyes, could imagine herself back in the Middle Ages, walking in that lovely parkland. There had been a house on this site even then.

She returned to the present century. The two women had been sorting out a timetable problem for the advanced maths group, who had important exams looming up. When that had been resolved, Miss Gates got up to go.

'That young man, Dennis Maxwell, has the right name,' she said suddenly. 'I think he's going to be a bit of a menace.'

'Really?' said Miss Welbeck, in surprise. 'I think we're lucky to have got him, Evelyn. He has much charm – and a brilliant mind.' She gave a teasing smile. 'His knowledge of new advances in the field of pure mathematics outstrips mine – and probably yours, too!'

'Why's he not got a permanent post somewhere then?'

Miss Welbeck gazed out of her window and smiled.

'He's young. He doesn't want to settle anywhere yet. He enjoys life! Trebizon's a very pleasant spot in the summer, especially when he has a girlfriend in the town here. He's quite a find, Evelyn! I'm sure the girls will respond to him.'

'I'm sure they will,' nodded Miss Gates, sagely.

'Dennis,' she muttered, as she left the room. 'Dennis the Menace.'

FIVE
Two Triumphs

Wednesday turned out very well in the end. After break, there was German with Herr Fischer. No one started German until the Second Year, so Rebecca was up with the rest. Then there was double French with Ma'm'selle Giscard, who always made her lessons interesting, when she remembered where they were. Dinner was only passable although the gravy was better than usual, but pudding was a light treacle sponge and custard – delicious. It was good to have Joss Vining back at the head of the table and she told Rebecca about the Athletics Club that met every Saturday afternoon in the summer term.

'I'll be joining that!' said Rebecca promptly.

She knew she could run well – but how well? She had never tested herself against proper competition.

This would be her chance to find out.

After lunch came chemistry with Mr Douglas, in the laboratory at the top of the modern block that housed the dining and assembly halls. Rebecca was at the bench nearest the window, where she could keep a watchful eye on the weather. The sun had gone in and a cool breeze had sprung up. She hoped it wouldn't rain, because the last lesson was double games and it seemed that in the summer term they did tennis on a Wednesday.

The rain held off and they were able to go out on to the courts in track suits. Rebecca loved tennis, both watching it on TV and trying to play it. But sometimes her play drove her to despair.

'Have you played much?' asked Miss Willis, the games mistress. She was sorting them out into fours. 'Have you had any coaching at *all*?'

'I've just played in the park with friends, in London.'

Rebecca was put in a four with three girls from Form II Gamma, Susan McTavish, Anne Brett and Jane O'Hara. They went to court nine and then they started to knock the ball to one another. Rebecca quickly realised that she had been put in a 'weak' group for although she hit the ball wildly and could never make it go where she wanted it to, she could at least hit it much harder than the other three. Susan McTavish kept skying the ball high into the air and Jane O'Hara couldn't get it over the net at all.

There was a great deal of hilarity, but for twenty minutes Rebecca's knowledge of the game remained at a standstill. All that changed when Miss Willis came striding over from court eight, where she had been teaching four girls backhand volley.

'You three are hopeless,' she said to Susan, Jane and Anne. 'You've forgotten everything you learnt last summer. As for you, Rebecca,' she walked up to her, 'has nobody ever taught you how to grip the racket for the forehand?'

She held out her right hand.

'Shake hands with me.'

Puzzled, Rebecca did so, while the other three giggled. Then Miss Willis took Rebecca's racket from her, held it by the head and proffered the handle.

'Now shake hands with your racket. A good, hard, firm handshake.'

As Rebecca obeyed, Miss Willis nodded in satisfaction.

'That's it. The forehand grip. That's all there is to it. Now, let me show you what you should do with your feet as you come up to make a forehand drive – be quiet, you three, and watch, you might learn something –'

Ten minutes later, Rebecca was hitting good low, straight forehands over the net every time Miss Willis threw a ball to her. It was unbelievable! It was like magic! It was all a matter of doing it the right way, instead of the wrong way.

'I've got to try and get round,' Miss Willis said then. 'The Sixth Form run tennis coaching sessions for the juniors, all through the summer term. I suggest you put your name down, Rebecca.'

'I will!' said Rebecca in delight. Five minutes later it began to pour with rain and they all dashed back to Juniper House.

With time to kill before tea, she and Tish and Sue went to the library, in old school, to do their English prep. They found Mara had got there ahead of them. She was poring over some reference books and making notes.

'It's for a history project we've been set,' explained Mara. The Beta form had already had their first history lesson of the term. 'I want to get an A.'

'You really *have* made up your mind, haven't you?' said Tish fondly. 'Hey, maybe it's a good thing you don't like surfing. At least there won't be that to distract you!'

'Surfing!' The very mention of it filled Rebecca with excitement. She walked over to the long elegant windows. The library was on the ground floor and overlooked the main forecourt of old school; it had once been the drawing room of the big house. The rain was beating against the windows now and the wind was getting up.

There wouldn't be any surfing this evening.

Tish and Sue joined her and they watched the rain.

'Look, isn't that Max's girlfriend?' said Rebecca. 'In that red sports car parked near the wall. Remember her on the beach last night? Gorgeous looking, isn't she!'

'She's come to pick him up after work!' said Sue.

'She's not wasting any time then,' said Tish, looking round at the library clock. 'Lessons aren't over yet –'

Even as she spoke, a bell began to ring outside,

signalling the end of afternoon lessons. It had scarcely finished reverberating when a figure came bounding out of the main school building, collar turned up against the rain, bulging briefcase in his hand. The girl at once threw open the passenger door of the sports car.

'Max isn't wasting any time either!' laughed Sue.

'Look!' exclaimed Rebecca. 'There's Roberta!'

Roberta Jones had appeared from nowhere, at a run, and headed Max off just before he could get into the car. She thrust an envelope into his hands, speaking eagerly, drops of rain running down her face. Max listened, smiled, nodded and took the envelope and stuck it under his jacket. His girlfriend, Kate, sounded the car horn noisily and Max promptly shunted Roberta off in the direction of the school and climbed into the car.

As it drove away, he waved to her and she waved back. There was a soppy look on her face and she hardly seemed aware of the rain.

'She was lying in wait for him!' giggled Sue.

'I wonder what was in that envelope?' asked Rebecca.

'A passionate love poem I expect,' snorted Tish. 'Gosh, he's soon going to get fed up with her if she carries on like this.'

They walked back to the long table where Mara was working and settled down alongside her and opened their English books. English was Rebecca's favourite subject, but now she couldn't settle down to her prep. She gave a heavy sigh.

'What's the matter?' asked Tish, always ready and eager to be distracted.

'Still can't understand that stuff about binary numbers. And he's going to test me tomorrow.'

Rebecca had been dipping into the maths text book all day, on and off, even in chemistry. She'd wanted to learn it and get it over with, especially as she'd thought there might be some surfing after tea.

'Oh, I thought you were going to say something interesting!' wailed Tish.

'This is the library!' said a prefect who had just come in. 'Don't make so much noise.'

'Come on, Rebeck!' Tish's voice dropped to a very low whisper. She pulled her chair close to Rebecca's and put an arm round her shoulders. 'Here, give me your English book.'

She carefully extracted the centre pages from Rebecca's English exercise book, picked up her pen, and wrote down 1111.

'Now in ordinary numbers, denary that is, those four figures'd be thousands, hundreds, tens and units,' she whispered. 'After the units column, everything is to the power of ten. 1111 is 1 plus 10^1 plus 10^2 plus 10^3. Well, with binary numbers, instead of thinking in powers of ten you think in powers of two, except in the units column.' She was writing figures down as she spoke. 'So 1111, when it's a binary number, become 1 plus 2^1 plus 2^2 plus 2^3. Work out what that is in ordinary numbers.'

She thrust the pen and paper in front of Rebecca, who frowned hard at what Tish had written down and thought about what she had been saying. She did some workings out and then scribbled an answer. Fifteen.

'That's right!' exclaimed Tish.

'Sssssh!' said the prefect.

Tish leant over and wrote some more numbers down. 'Now try those!' she mouthed. Rebecca worked away in silence. As she got each answer correct, Tish grinned and put a thumb up. A feeling of relief swept over Rebecca. The book made it seem so difficult. But it was easy when someone explained it properly. Like that tennis forehand!

She'd just finished when the first tea bell rang.

They all left their prep in the library and rushed outside. They'd have to come back and finish it after tea. Right now, they were hungry – and happy, especially Rebecca.

'Thanks!' she said to Tish. 'I still can't believe it's that simple! What do we need to know them for anyway?'

'Search me,' grinned Tish. 'Why do we need to know how to find the area of a trapezium, or how to prove triangles are congruent . . .'

'If you're an acrobat-ium,' said Sue, keeping a straight face, 'it's *vital* you know the area of a trapezium.'

'Arrgh.' They all groaned at such a terrible joke. But it was Mara, surprisingly, who answered Rebecca's question.

'Binary numbers are needed for computers,' she said. 'It means you can take any number at all and break it down into just ones and noughts. The computers prefer it that way!'

'Any number at all?' Rebecca thought about it for a moment. 'Yes, I suppose you can. Mara, you're brilliant! Have you had a brain transplant in the holidays?'

Mara shrieked and threw her history book at

Rebecca. Rebecca ducked and it hit the wall, just as a prefect came round the corner.

'Pick that book up and go across and have your tea. Don't run! Walk.'

Yes, today had turned out well, Rebecca decided as she drank her cocoa in the Common Room, just before bedtime. She had marvellous friends and a lot of things to look forward to.

She walked across to the noticeboard and looked at Roberta's play announcement. Only three people had signed up to be in it – Debbie Rickard and Sarah and Ruth Nathan. It was a shame, really. Poor old Roberta!

Roberta Jones created a minor sensation on Thursday morning. She arrived for breakfast wearing her hair loose. Rebecca had never seen her in anything but thick, droopy plaits before. Now her hair cascaded round her shoulders, brown and gleaming and well-brushed.

'Ye gods,' said Tish, as Roberta took her seat at the next table.

'It's maths first lesson,' observed Sue calmly.

It got the day off to a merry start, though Roberta was going to spring a much bigger surprise than that before the day was out.

It was another good day for Rebecca, in fact it was a superlative day, because it was on Thursday afternoon that she really got the hang of surfing.

Once again, the only jarring note of the day was struck by the maths lesson. Rebecca was almost looking forward to being tested on binary numbers, now she understood them. But Max forgot all about her. After handing them back their maths exercise books – and Rebecca's had a large red nought written on it – Max pressed straight on to talk about factorising. This was something else that Rebecca had never done. Max rattled on about it at such speed that she still only half understood it when he wrote up an exercise on the blackboard and told them to get on with it.

Rebecca kept putting her hand up but although he briefly answered questions from Anne Finch and Aba Amori and Margot Lawrence, he just ignored her. Finally he settled down for another long session with Roberta. They seemed to be going through something together. At the time, Rebecca assumed it was yesterday's binary numbers and that Roberta had still managed to get them wrong.

'She's hopeless, isn't she?' whispered Sue. 'Come

on, I'll help you.'

With Sue's help, Rebecca managed to do four of the ten questions on the board. Then the bell went and they had to hand their books in for marking.

The sun broke through the clouds just before dinner time and after that the friends could talk of nothing but surfing. It was double games again in the afternoon and on Thursdays, Tish told Rebecca, they could choose between several activities – including going in the sea, if they had their swimming certificates and the weather was good enough, with Harry supervising them.

Mara managed to get excused from games because she wanted to finish her history project ('Isn't she keen!' said someone) but the other five members of the Action Committee couldn't wait to get down to the beach and into wetsuits. They needed plenty of practice if they were going to raise a lot of money doing a Sponsored Surf for Charity Week. As for Rebecca, she was determined to master the art. Then she could get some sponsorships and be in it with the other four.

'Elf, you amaze me!' she shouted as the plump girl came streaking past her on her Malibu board, heading inshore, while she was still hard at work paddling hers out to beyond the breaker line. Sue, Tish and Margot rode in just behind Elf, on the next breaker. They stood on their boards in a line like circus bareback riders – experts, all of them! *'Come on, Rebeck!'*

Gasping for breath, the salt spray in her face, lying tight to her board, Rebecca got out behind the breakers at last. She turned, gripped the board and waited for a big wave. As it came, she missed her footing on the Malibu and instead of riding in with the wave, it washed right over her. But she was still holding her board. The next wave came, not quite so big – she took it!

Gloriously, Rebecca felt herself being lifted high in the air. Like a tightrope walker she struggled to an upright position, arms outstretched, legs wobbling, getting her weight distributed evenly on the board . . . now it felt right! She was shooting in on the breaker at speed – it was sensational fun – she wasn't going to fall off this time! It was all a matter of balance.

'I can do it! I can do it!' she cried as she glided into the shallows. The others were holding their boards aloft, cheering her. Harry came wading into the water to meet her, smiling broadly.

'You're a natural, you are. You're well away now!'

'I can do it!' Rebecca said, yet again.

It was a moment of sweet triumph.

Roberta Jones's triumph – her big surprise – was yet to come.

The gang from dormitory six had enjoyed their surfing so much that they collared Mara afterwards and walked along to the Hobbies Room in Juniper House. 'You'd better help with the sponsorship form, Mara,' said Tish, 'as you're going to be the steward. Say how you'd like it set out and I'll type it out on a stencil skin. Then we can run all the forms off on the duplicator straight after tea.'

'And start finding people to sponsor us!' said Rebecca eagerly. She'd made six successful surf-rides in all. Now she was confident that she could take part. 'Some of the First Years are planning to have a Sponsored Walk.'

'We'd better get in quickly then!' said Margot. 'We don't want everyone pledging their money to them first!'

But when they entered the Hobbies Room, they found that Roberta Jones was using the typewriter. Sarah Nathan was reading a typescript to her and Roberta was laboriously transcribing it on to a stencil skin. She had already completed four stencils and this was the fifth. Ruth Nathan was fixing the first stencil up on to the duplicator. Debbie Rickard was hanging round watching. There was a general air of suppressed excitement.

'They've been here all afternoon,' Verity Williams told them, in a whisper. She was painting a water-colour in the Art Corner. 'Miss Morgan got them off games so they could do this.'

'How long are you going to be with the typewriter, Robert?' asked Tish, marching over. 'We need it for something.'

'Hours yet,' replied Roberta happily. 'We're duplicating my play. Miss Morgan's given permission.'

'Come on,' said Rebecca, taking Tish by the arm. 'Let's just rough out the sponsorship form somewhere. We can run it off tomorrow.'

'It's nearly tea time anyway,' said Sue. 'I'm starving.'

'It's the magazine meeting after tea,' remembered Margot.

'What on earth's she getting her play duplicated for?' exploded Tish, once they were out in the corridor. 'She's already had a lot of copies typed out in the holidays. Now she's running it off on the duplicator. Nobody wants to be in it, in any case.'

'Maybe she thinks they will if it's printed!' laughed Mara.

Rebecca was very surprised when Roberta didn't turn up for the magazine meeting, later. Jenny was there with her wire tray, collecting in contributions for *The Trebizon Journal* from girls who had brought them. She then told the assembled First Years and Second Years that they still had a fortnight to submit something and they'd better try hard because this would be Audrey Maxwell's last issue. Roberta Jones turned up right at the end of the meeting.

'Hallo,' said Jenny, in a resigned voice. 'Have you got something?'

Roberta was usually the first person to plonk something in the wire tray. Every term she tried to get something shortlisted for *The Trebizon Journal*. But this time she just waved her hand, airily.

'Sorry, Jenny. Too busy. I just wondered if I might make a quick announcement. While there's a good crowd here.'

'Go ahead.'

'Well,' said Roberta, taking a deep breath, 'it's about my play.' People began to fidget but Roberta raised her voice. 'I know a lot of you haven't had time to sign up for tomorrow's auditions.' Everyone giggled at that word *auditions*. 'Well, don't bother to sign up, just come along. And by the way,' she backed towards the door of the Common Room and made her dramatic exit line:

'In case you think the play isn't much good, you might like to know that Mr Maxwell likes it very much and has agreed to act as producer. In fact he'll be taking tomorrow's meeting.'

She left behind her a stunned silence.

Rebecca's moment of triumph in Trebizon Bay had been sweet. But Roberta's was even sweeter.

<u>SIX</u>
Looking Forward to Charity Week

'He must be mad,' said Sue, for about the tenth time, as the whole dormitory discussed it, long after lights out. 'Fancy wanting to produce *A Midsummer Night's Nightmare* or whatever it's called.'

'Stark, staring mad,' agreed Elf, who had read the play.

'I think I'll go along all the same,' giggled Joanna Thompson, up in the corner. 'This should be funny.'

'Who won't be going along?' said Rebecca, sleepily. 'I mean, who's going to miss this? I can't wait!'

Similar conversations were taking place all over Juniper House, with the result that the Second Year Common Room was packed out for Roberta's play meeting the next day, more packed than Rebecca had ever seen it. In fact the six of them hadn't bothered to rush over their school dinner, and now found it quite impossible to get in. They joined the jostling throng in the corridor, crowding round the door, up on tiptoes to try and get a look.

Max was taking the meeting, standing behind a table at the top end of the room. Roberta was seated demurely beside him. The freshly-stencilled copies of the play had already been handed out, one between three, and were being eagerly read. Just inside the door, Jenny Brook-Hayes had managed to get one and was flicking through it rapidly.

'Still the same play, Jenny?' asked Sue in a loud whisper.

'No fear!' said Jenny. 'He's just about rewritten it!'

Max began to speak loudly and the room fell quiet.

'This play is going to be a lot of fun and I'm sure it'll raise a lot of money for Charity Week. So here's a chance for any girl who likes acting and isn't already fixed up in a group, to do her bit. Bobbie and I have decided to change the title to A Woodland Comedy.'

'It was a tragedy before!' Sally Elphinstone hissed

to Rebecca, on the verge of laughter.

'You've rewritten it, sir,' piped up a First Year girl in the room.

'No, no, not at all,' said Max, glancing at Roberta. 'Just a few minor changes, with Bobbie's permission. We've cut down the number of parts to ten and introduced a little light-hearted dialogue.'

Roberta nodded happily. She was wearing her hair loose for the second day running.

'By the way,' Max continued, 'it occurred to me that the play should be performed in the open air and that South Terrace by the Music School would be the perfect setting. The trees and lake there will give us the rustic atmosphere, in fact it makes a perfect open-air theatre – as long as the weather's kind to us –'

They laughed as they looked at the rain beating on the windows.

His enthusiasm was infectious. A stir of interest was running round the room. When he asked how many people would like to be in the play about twenty hands shot up. 'Okay, everyone who's put their hand up had better take a copy of the play away with them. Look at it carefully. We'll have another meeting after school and hold auditions. Where do you suggest, Bobbie –?'

He turned to her deferentially.

'I'll ask Miss Willis if we can use the gym, shall I?' said Roberta.

'For those who don't get a part in the play, there'll be plenty of other jobs,' said Max. 'We'll need help with props and costumes and –'

'Come on,' said Tish, as the meeting continued. 'I'm getting a crick in my neck. Let's do the sponsorship form now, shall we?'

'We've heard enough!' said Mara, with a smile.

As they moved off down the corridor Rebecca heard Debbie Rickard's voice raised in the meeting:

'Please, Max, I've already been given the part of fairy queen. Roberta promised it to me.'

They all laughed and jostled and shoved each other down the stairs to the Hobbies Room on the ground floor. They were very impressed, all the same.

'So that's what she gave him on Wednesday!' said Rebecca. 'Her play. She must have asked him for suggestions.'

'He rewrote it and then they went through it together, in the lesson yesterday morning!' Tish realised. 'He was showing her all the changes.'

'But fancy him agreeing to produce it as well!' said Margot. 'It'll be good now! Roberta's group will probably raise the most money.'

'Not if we can help it!' said Tish, pushing open the door of the Hobbies Room. 'Come on, let's get this form worked out and then I'll make a stencil for it.'

Mara worked out a layout quickly and Tish just managed to finish typing the stencil when the bell went for afternoon school. First lesson was physics and then there would be double games.

'We'll come back straight after games and run it off on the duplicator. There's room for ten sponsors on each form and as we'll each want to try and get loads, we'd better have several forms each.'

The weather was very bad again, so although Friday was another tennis afternoon, it was called off and the girls did PE in the gym, instead. Rebecca was disappointed about that. Obviously there would be no surfing that evening, either. Well, they could get the forms run off and start collecting some sponsorships, instead.

They had showers after the PE lesson, and before leaving the sports centre Rebecca looked back in the gym. She saw that Roberta was arranging chairs

in a big circle. She was getting everything ready for
Max and company. She usually looked so stolid but
now, with her hair loose and a soft expression on
her face, she looked quite different.

On the way back, Rebecca and Tish met Sue
outside the Hilary. Sue had orchestra practice on
Friday afternoons, instead of games. They looked
across at South Terrace, on the far side of the Music
School. It was framed by trees that overhung the
waters of the little lake. The leaves were dripping
after the recent downpours, but as she gazed
dreamily at the scene, Rebecca could imagine it in
sunshine, peopled by goblins and elves and a fairy
queen.

'You've got to hand it to Max,' she said. 'It'll make a lovely setting for the play. I bet a lot of people will turn up.'

Max's girlfriend wasn't very pleased about the play.

Rebecca discovered that quite by accident. When they got to the Hobbies Room they found that Roberta had used up the last of the duplicating paper and they needed some more. It was kept in a cupboard in the school office and Rebecca offered to run over to the old building and get some. If Mrs Devenshire had gone home she wouldn't mind them taking some. Rebecca had often done it before, on a Sunday. They always seemed to run out of paper on Sunday evenings, in the middle of printing *The Juniper Journal*!

The door of the school office was ajar. Rebecca was about to go in when she heard Max's voice. He had nipped in to use the phone! She hung around in the corridor, waiting for him to come out. He and Katie were having a shouting match.

'I did *not* spend all evening on that play, I spent about an hour on it . . . and only because it was a mess . . .' Then: 'Look, Katie, be reasonable, the kids are trying to raise some money for charity. They need some help with this play. Yes, sure it means staying late a few afternoons . . . but the whole thing'll be over in a fortnight . . . sorry, Katie. I've said I'll do it now and that's that. I'll see you later.'

As Rebecca heard the phone slam down, she walked heavily up to the door, as though she'd just that minute arrived. She marched in as Max marched out. He hardly noticed her. He just went off down the corridor with long, easy strides, his dark hair looking rather rumpled. He was whistling.

After she'd had tea and done her prep, Rebecca wandered round Juniper House collecting up sponsorships. Josselyn Vining was amazed that she'd learnt to surf so quickly and signed up her name on Rebecca's form, pledging two pence for each ride Rebecca could make before she fell off.

'Who'll be there to see you don't cheat?'

'Well Mara will be keeping score, as she doesn't like surfing, but Joanne Hissup is drafting in some prefects as well. They'll supervise and double-check. It should turn into quite a contest between Tish and Margot!'

'Could I be in it, too?' asked Joss suddenly. 'I was going to run a cake stall with Jenny and Co., but the wretches have gone and got themselves in this play!'

'I'm sure you can, Joss!' said Rebecca in delight. 'I'll ask the others when I see them.'

'Don't forget Athletics Club's tomorrow afternoon,' the junior school head of games said, as she walked away. 'Let's see what your sprinting times are like.'

Rebecca had no intention of forgetting.

That night, in the dormitory, Jenny Brook-Hayes and Joanna Thompson confessed that they had gone along to the second play meeting, just for interest. But the auditions had been such fun, they'd decided to join in, and Max had given them each a part. They were slightly shamefaced about it.

'We found out that some of the First Years are planning a cake stall, anyway.'

'No point in duplicating.'

'Of course not!' said Tish. 'Let's face it, the play's going to be quite good now.'

She was feeling happy because Joss was going to join them in the Sponsored Surf. It was a feather in their caps. What a contest it would be now! A big crowd would come to watch and that meant they should be able to pull in a lot of last-minute sponsorships on the day.

'Have you noticed, Becky, Robert's suddenly got

nicer,' Tish said, at bedtime. They were both gazing out of the window by Rebecca's bed. 'She came up to me at cocoa time – and you know how you have to twist everyone's arm – well, she offered to sponsor me, without me even asking! Two pence a ride!'

'I had noticed,' said Rebecca. She gazed out at the night sky. The heavy cloud that had lain above Trebizon Bay all day had now cleared away and she could see the stars quite clearly. 'It's obvious why.'

'Yes,' said Tish. 'Somebody really likes her writing at last.'

'I wish Max liked me,' Rebecca said with a sigh. The maths lesson that morning had been yet another disaster. Max had demonstrated a lot of instructive games they could play with calculators. The only trouble was that Rebecca didn't have a calculator. When it came to setting 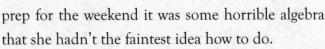 prep for the weekend it was some horrible algebra that she hadn't the faintest idea how to do.

'Don't think about maths,' said Tish.

'Don't worry, I'm not going to,' replied Rebecca.

There were too many other things to think about. All of them were preferable to maths.

SEVEN
All Set

It was a hectic weekend. It was so hectic that Rebecca completely forgot to do her maths prep. She remembered it late on Sunday evening, just before she fell asleep, by which time it was too late to do anything about it.

The weather was good that weekend. The rainclouds had disappeared and clear blue skies and sunshine appeared, to welcome in the month of May.

'I've got a feeling it's going to be a long, hot summer,' said Tish after breakfast on Saturday morning. 'Wouldn't that be nice?'

'Yes,' nodded Rebecca. At the end of spring term she'd joined the Gardening Club. She'd planted seeds in her own patch in the walled kitchen gardens at the back of the stable block. Sometime over the weekend she must go and see how they were getting on! A sunny May coming after a fairly wet April would do them the world of good.

'What are you two doing after we've seen the film?' asked Tish.

'I'm going to the Hilary,' said Sue. 'Mr Barrington wants to see all the Music Scholars at eleven o'clock. It's something to do with a Youth Music Festival in the summer holidays.'

Life was exciting for Sue since she'd been elected one of the school's Music Scholars at the end of last term.

'I've got my first tennis coaching!' said Rebecca. 'I'm in Pippa's group and we're to meet on court number three.'

'I'll do my prep maybe,' said Tish.

First they went to see the film, in the assembly hall. All the juniors had been ordered to go. It was followed by a talk. Although most of Juniper House turned up, a few girls had skived off because it was such a lovely morning. If it had been Walt Disney or Laurel and Hardy it might have been different, but this film was called *Animals need Real Kindness* and had a serious message throughout.

Animals need Real Kindness, ARK for short, was a well-known charity. It was never easy to decide which charity should benefit from the special fundraising week that the juniors organised each May. There were so many deserving causes. This year ARK had been chosen and now the charity's west country organiser, a lady called Julia White, had come to show the film to the girls and talk to them afterwards.

It was a good charity, efficiently run, with the aim of alleviating any kind of unnecessary suffering amongst animals. The film *Animals need Real Kindness* showed the wide range of its activities. These included providing free vets for people too poor to have their pets made better, saving old horses and looking after animals that had been neglected or ill-treated. Some parts of the film brought Rebecca close to tears, especially the sight of a tiny puppy that had been abandoned and would have died if it hadn't been brought to an ARK centre in the nick of time.

'The whole school should have come!' whispered Sue indignantly, as soon as the film had ended. 'Then they'd really want to give all the cash they've got to Charity Week.'

'We ought to write it up in *The J.J.!*' said Tish at once. 'We're compiling a list of the fundraising events. We ought to describe ARK properly – this film and everything.'

'Yes!' said Mara. 'Let's ask Susannah what she thinks.'

The juniors' weekly news-sheet, *The Juniper Journal*, was produced by an editorial committee of three consisting of Mara, Tish and Susannah Skelhorn, who represented the First Years and collected in all their contributions. Tish typed the stencils and they printed it on the duplicator on Sunday evenings, front and back of a single sheet of paper, to be sold around the school for five pence a copy on Monday. It even had quite a good sale in the Staff Room.

'Rebecca must write it,' said Susannah when Tish ran over to her. 'She's the best writer.'

Mrs Beal, about to introduce the speaker, clapped her hands for order. Tish ran back to her seat and spoke quickly behind her hand.

'Ask questions at the end, Rebeck. Write it all down.'

'Okay!' said Rebecca, feeling flustered and pleased. She found some scraps of paper in the pocket of her skirt and Sue produced a ballpoint pen. After that, she carefully noted down points from the charity worker's talk and asked two questions at the end, feeling like a proper reporter. Sue also stood up and asked a question:

'Can you tell us how much one pound could do and how much five pounds could do and how much ten pounds could do?'

'That's a very good question,' said Julia White. 'I'll give you some examples.'

Rebecca wrote them down as quickly as she could. That would fit in well to the piece she was going to write.

For the rest of the morning she kept planning out what she would say. It was there in the back of her mind, all the time, even when she was at tennis coaching.

'Throw the ball up straight, Rebecca. You'll never, never have a good service if you don't learn to throw the ball up straight.'

'Sorry, Pippa.'

But at the end of the session she was surprised and faintly excited when Pippa took her aside for a moment and said:

'Rebecca Mason, I think you might make a tennis

player one day.'

'Me?'

'Yes, you. Practise throwing things up straight whenever you can. Just use a shoe, anything that's handy. See you next Saturday?'

'Yes!'

Rebecca wrote her first rough draft in the dinner hour. It was rushed and a bit of a jumble, but she wanted to get her thoughts down about ARK and why it was important. She mustn't make it boring! She badly wanted all the people who hadn't been to the film to read about it and not just skip over it. Juniper House wanted their pocket money: this was the reason why! Once she'd got something down on paper she felt better and she hurried off to the Athletics Club.

The Club meeting was the high point of the day. The school was lucky. Angela Hessel, who had twice represented Great Britain in the pentathlon in the Olympic Games, actually lived near Trebizon these days with her husband and three children. She came in as Athletics Coach every summer term. For most of the afternoon she was busy coaching some of the seniors in the high jump – Joanne Hissup, the senior Head of Games, was regarded as an England prospect. While that was going on, Joss Vining timed Rebecca's running over four different distances – 100 metres, 200 metres, 400 metres and 800 metres. That just confirmed what they'd guessed. Rebecca was best at sprinting, not the middle distances.

At the end of the afternoon Angela Hessel spent five whole minutes with her, showing her how to start from blocks. Rebecca practised starting for a while and then did the 100 metres again. Tish timed her this time.

'What did I do?' gasped Rebecca after she'd crossed the 100 metres line, slowing down and looking back over her shoulder.

'Fourteen seconds!' yelled Tish, looking at the stopwatch.

'Is that good?' asked Rebecca. Heaving for breath, she walked back to pick her track suit up off the grass. 'I'm shattered. I thought I was quite fit, but I can't be.'

'Nobody is at the beginning of term,' said Judy Sharp coming over from the long jump pit. She watched Rebecca put her track suit on over her shorts and blue tee shirt. Athletics Club was over for the afternoon. 'What time did she do, Tish?'

'Fourteen.'

'Hey, that's quite good for a start!'

'Is it really quite good?' asked Rebecca as they walked away from the sports field. Tish liked distance running and had spent the afternoon fairly gently, just jogging round and round the track. 'What do you think?'

'Yes. You only have to do 13.5 seconds and you'll qualify for the junior 100 metres on Sports Day.'

'When is Sports Day?' asked Rebecca.

'Friday before half-term. A lot of parents come

down for it and then take us back home afterwards. Will yours –?'

One look at Rebecca's face was enough. Her parents were due for two months' leave in the summer, but they'd still be in Saudi Arabia at the end of May. She would have liked them to come to Sports Day!

'13.5?' repeated Rebecca, when the miserable feeling had subsided.

Silently she vowed that, parents or no parents, she was going to qualify for the 100 metres sprint on Sports Day – and the 200 metres, too!

'The Junior record's 12.4,' Tish added casually. 'Get near that and you'd go through to the Area Sports after half-term, then probably the County Sports at the end of term.'

'Let's go and find Sue,' Rebecca said, changing the subject. 'She's probably finished playing tennis by now. Let's all have some fizzy at Moffatt's.'

From that moment onwards, Rebecca decided that although she wanted to learn how to play tennis properly, and surf-riding was the most exciting new thing she had ever done, only one thing really mattered this term. She wanted to run in the County Sports, at the end of term, when her parents would be back in England to see her!

She spent Saturday evening in the library, alone. She wanted it that way. After rushing through some French prep as fast as she possibly could, she worked on the piece about ARK. One of the problems was getting it all into 400 words, which was the most she could be allowed in the little news-sheet. She polished the phrases up, rewrote some bits and cut others. At last she was satisfied with it. The bedtime bell was going. She would copy it out neatly some time tomorrow and then hand it to Tish to go into *The Juniper Journal*.

Sunday morning the weather was still fine and they went surfing after church and before Sunday lunch. The sunshine and clear skies were deceptive for the breakers were much higher than they'd been on Thursday afternoon, when Rebecca had done so well. She kept coming off her Malibu board at first, but she finished the morning with two glorious rides.

'I hope the waves aren't as high as that on the day we do it,' she said to Margot afterwards. 'I won't raise a penny if I come off first time, like this morning.'

'You'll be all right if you keep practising!' said Margot, droplets of salt water on her gleaming skin.

They saw Roberta Jones coming back across the sands with Sarah and Ruth Nathan. They'd been for a walk right across the bay. Shading her eyes and looking into the distance, Rebecca saw the reason. Max was surfing on the far side of the bay on his unmistakable red Malibu board. They had been to watch him.

They all met Mara as they went into the dining hall. In contrast to their healthy open-air glow she looked frowsy and her large brown eyes lacked their usual lustre. She had spent the morning on some difficult prep, determined to get good marks for it.

On Sunday afternoon Rebecca copied out her piece for *The J.J.* and took it along to the Hobbies Room. Tish was busy sorting out all the material that Mara and Susannah had gathered up, putting it into some sort of order. Then she would begin to type the stencils. Her sister had taught her how to type properly which was how she came to be editor of *The J.J.* Susannah, who was very good at art, was roughing out a layout for the news-sheet with some possible headlines such as: BEST EVER CHARITY WEEK PLANNED and START SAVING YOUR MONEY NOW. It had been decided to turn the whole issue over to Charity Week, with a complete list of all the events that the First and Second Years were planning.

'Hey, this is you at your best,' said Tish, quickly reading through Rebecca's piece. 'This should come first, before anything else, with a really eye-catching headline. Something like: ANIMALS NEED REAL KINDNESS – DON'T READ THIS IF YOU'RE SQUEAMISH.'

When the issue went on sale on Monday, a lot of people congratulated Tish – and Rebecca – but not Debbie Rickard. She came up at morning break with Roberta Jones.

'Fancy putting that gruesome piece in as the main story. You know full well the play's the big story – but you've just shoved it in a list with all the other things that are happening. You jealous or something?'

'Shut up, you silly fool,' was Tish's comment.

Debbie took it for granted that Roberta felt the way she did. She was amazed when Roberta suddenly touched Rebecca's arm.

'It's a beautiful piece,' she said. 'Now the whole school will known what Charity Week's all about this year.'

'Hasn't she changed!' whispered Sue, as the pair walked away.

'It's Max,' said Tish.

Rebecca smiled. But she was touched. It made her hard work seem worthwhile. She was even more touched in maths, which was the first lesson after break, when Roberta said:

'*Don't* give her a penalty mark, Max! She really didn't have time to do her prep. She was writing up something for Charity Week, a lovely piece about . . .'

But for once Max cut Roberta short.

'I don't care if Rebecca was writing the Domesday Book. She was supposed to do some algebra.'

During the next two weeks the excitement in Juniper House increased as Charity Week drew near. In spite of rain, and Athletics Club was cancelled two Saturdays running, Rebecca got some more surfing in. She was getting quite good at the art of remaining upright on a speeding Malibu board. Battling against tough opposition from those First Years who were organising a sponsored walk, Rebecca managed to get thirty-four sponsors in all. She worked out that she would raise, in one and two pences, forty pence for each ride she could make before she either fell off or got exhausted. Two of the others had done even better. Joss would be making forty-six pence a ride! Their great ambition still was to raise more money than any other group, even the play crowd.

During the fortnight, maths lessons were a riot. There were nine girls in II Alpha involved with the play, one half of the class. At every opportunity they sidetracked Max into talking about it. There was a kind of carnival atmosphere in the air. Once Miss Gates walked in just as Max was demonstrating to Judy Sharp how to do a little goblin dance. She silenced the hilarity with an unusual display of anger.

'I am trying to give a lesson in the next room!' she said to the girls. At Max she directed a look that would have withered the sun. He became very brisk and strict for the rest of the lesson.

Rebecca enjoyed these diversions as much as anyone, but she felt uneasy, sometimes, come evening when she was struggling with maths prep. She always seemed to be doing things wrong again.

'Don't worry,' said Sue once. 'Everything'll settle down once Charity Week's over.'

The surfing gang were overjoyed when it was agreed that the Sponsored Surf should take place on Sunday morning. So it would be the very first event of the Week!

They suffered agonies on the Saturday when wind and rain came. They'd put up posters all over the school and they knew that plenty of people wanted to come, especially to see Joss, Tish and Margot fighting it out. It was bound to develop into a marathon between these three, long after the others had dropped out. How many pounds might they not raise between them! But if the weather was bad the whole thing would have to be postponed until later in the week when there would be counter-attractions, including prep.

To their utter relief, Sunday morning dawned clear.

Tish and Rebecca went down to the beach early and planted a big banner they had made: SUPPORT THE SPONSORED SURF FOR ARK. The bay was deserted and the waves rolled in long, unbroken lines of white foam on to golden sand. Perfect conditions! They heard a faint cry high above them. For a moment Rebecca thought it was a seagull and then, looking up, she saw a solitary hang-glider sailing past, high above them. The cry came again and it sounded like 'Good luck!'

'It's Max – it must be!' exclaimed Tish, staring upwards.

They both waved feverishly, laughing in delight.

'Nothing can go wrong now!' exclaimed Rebecca. 'Even Max is on our side.'

'Not to mention over your head as usual!'

He went drifting gently onwards, towards a patch of rosy sky.

EIGHT
The Bitter End

'We've even had a visitation from the sky!' Tish said to the others, as they all went down to the beach at nine o'clock. 'A guardian angel flew over!'

There was excited laughter. Max belonged to the Hang-Gliding Club over at Mulberry but no one had actually seen him airborne until today. It was just the right, zany start to what proved to be a wonderful morning.

The six surfers got there early and changed into wetsuits. Dozens of girls from the school, as well as members of staff, were soon joined by local people and some early holidaymakers about in Trebizon Bay. They all gathered around the big banner and waited.

Mara had some spare forms down on the

beach and Rebecca and Co. moved amongst the bystanders, collecting more signatures.

'How long have you been surfing?' asked a good-looking boy whom Rebecca had noticed around the town occasionally. He was preparing to sign her form, tapping his chin with the end of a pencil.

'Less than three weeks!' said Rebecca.

'Is that all? Then I bet you don't do more than three rides without falling off!' He laughed. 'Here, I'll sponsor you for three pence a ride.'

'Thanks,' said Rebecca, demurely, determined to surprise him.

She found seven more sponsors at a penny a ride, bringing the money pledged up to a grand total of fifty pence a ride. What an incentive to do well! Joss managed to get her total up to eighty pence a ride.

Everything was ready. Mara and a prefect called Della Thomas were up on high umpire chairs, borrowed from the tennis courts. The chairs stood squarely on the sand, looking out to sea. As stewards, they had blue cards on which they'd tick off the number of rides each girl made. Joanna Hissup herself had turned up and took charge of the metal cash box, so that money could be collected quickly from the new sponsors, as soon as a girl's score was known.

'All set?' Harry blew his whistle. 'Go!'

The six girls ran into the water, splashing and laughing and holding their Malibu boards aloft. As soon as the water was above the waist they jumped themselves flat on to their boards and paddled furiously with their hands to get out beyond the breaker line.

'The waves are breaking miles out today!' gasped Rebecca to Sue, who was alongside her, looking different without her glasses. 'It's going to take longer to get out!'

'Longer rides coming in!' yelled Sue eagerly.

'Long enough to fall off, too!' shouted Rebecca, in some trepidation. She thought of all the people watching from the shore. Now that the moment had come she dreaded making a fool of herself. Supposing she fell off on her first ride? Then she would have to come out – without having raised a single penny for ARK. 'Look at those three!'

Margot, Tish and Joss were forging ahead. They were almost out beyond the breakers. Elf wasn't very far behind them. Rebecca redoubled her efforts, battling through the spray. This was going to be the hardest part, getting out each time!

Rebecca rose to the occasion. Tish, Margot and Joss made a superb first ride in, all in a line, and a cheer went up for them. Sue, Rebecca and Elf followed a few breakers later, not quite so expert, and a bit raggedy-looking, but they made it and another cheer went up! Elf raised a hand to acknowledge the cheers and slipped off the Malibu at the water's edge, but no-one counted that as a fall.

'I've raised fifty pence!' thought Rebecca in relief, turning round and heading straight back out to sea again. 'Now for the next one!'

By the eighth ride, Rebecca was exhausted, but she hadn't come off yet. This time, though, she wobbled badly, halfway back to shore. Her arms flailed round and round like windmill sails as she fought to keep upright on the speeding board. Then, nerve-rackingly, she steadied herself and managed to complete the ride. A crowd of First Years shouted and cheered.

On the ninth ride a big breaker took her up before she had properly got her balance and tossed Rebecca in one direction and the Malibu in another. It was all over! She shook the water out of her eyes and minutes later carried the Malibu on her back, up the sandy shore, to cheers intermingled with a slow handclap. She was first out. But she hadn't disgraced herself by any means. The nice boy came up.

'You've been doing it more than three weeks, I bet!' But he was smiling and digging his hand into his pocket. 'Who do I give the twenty-four pence to, anyway?'

'That tall girl with the cash box, please.'

In spite of the sun, Rebecca felt cold and rushed to change in the end beach hut. She mustn't miss the rest of the contest!

As she came out, Miss Morgan had hot soup ready for her and she gulped it gratefully. Nothing had ever tasted so delicious!

'Well done, Rebecca. How much have you raised?'

'Four pounds!' It wasn't just the soup that was making her glow. 'Four whole pounds!'

'The first four pounds of Charity Week!' the House Mistress pointed out, as Rebecca handed back the empty carton.

It was an exciting contest. Elf dropped out after twelve rides, too tired to go on. Then Sue got a slight attack of cramp after her thirteenth ride and came straight out. Now, as everyone had expected, the marathon developed between Joss and Tish and Margot. Joss was piling up rides faster than the other two by getting out more quickly. After her sixteenth ride she stood in the shallows, recovering her breath and arching her back, hands on her hips.

'Out, Joss!' shouted Joanne Hissup. 'That's enough.'

There were a few boos as Joss came out because some of the local boys had started laying bets amongst themselves and three of them had backed her to win. But Rebecca could tell from the way Joss was walking that her back had stiffened up slightly. It wasn't so very long since her spell in hospital.

'I can go on a long time yet,' she protested.

'You can, but you're not going to,' said Joanne.

That left Tish and Margot to battle it out. Soon they had overtaken Joss's score of sixteen rides. Seventeen . . . eighteen . . . nineteen . . .

'Surely they can't go on much longer!' Rebecca said to Sue.

'They can!' said Sue. 'Look at their faces. Neither of them wants to be the first to give in. At this rate, Harry will just have to blow his whistle and – oh! Tish!'

It was over. A moment's loss of concentration on her twentieth ride and Tish keeled off her board and Margot went shooting ahead of her with a yell of triumph. 'I've won!' she cried. Loud cheers went up and then Harry really did blow his whistle. It was time for Sunday lunch.

After dinner, Mara checked all the sponsorship forms against the number of rides and did a lot of calculations on a piece of paper. The gang were lying sleepily around the Common Room, mainly on the floor.

'We've raised forty-nine pounds and twenty

pence!' she announced. They all cheered. 'Now I'm going to check it with my calculator.'

'Well?' they asked excitedly, when she'd pressed all the buttons.

'It's still forty-nine pounds twenty,' said Mara in delight. 'I shall come into III Alpha next term, you see. Just wait and see if I don't.'

Later in the afternoon, Tish and Mara vanished into the Hobbies Room with Susannah Skelhorn to get *The Juniper Journal* ready. Rebecca's regular 'Did-You-Know?' piece wasn't needed because the weekly sheet was again crowded out with Charity Week news. So she and Sue and Elf and Margot spent the rest of Sunday collecting up sponsorship money in the metal cash box.

It was easy to find people because Juniper House was full of Middle School and Senior girls supporting the first day of Charity Week. Cakes were being sold at the cake stall, Hoop-la and darts and roll-a-penny had been set up in the First Year Common Room and Verity Williams was doing lightning portraits for ten pence a time.

A lot of the sponsors were surprised at the amount they owed, especially those who'd recklessly promised a penny or even two pence a ride to people like Tish and Margot. Roberta Jones could hardly believe she owed thirty-eight pence! Some of the First Years, especially, looked worried – like Sheila Cummings and her friend Eleanor Keating.

'Can I pay half now and half next Saturday, when Morgy pays out next week's allowance?' wailed Sheila. 'If I pay it all now I'll have nothing left for anything else!'

'We wouldn't even have enough to go and see the play on Friday!' added Eleanor.

'Of course,' smiled Rebecca. 'A lot of people are doing that. If you're really going to be skint, you can leave it all till next Saturday. Cheer up!'

By evening the friends had collected up almost twenty-four pounds, with the rest promised for the following Saturday. The box felt beautifully heavy. Rebecca put her head round the corner of the Hobbies Room and told Tish. 'Late news! We've already got in twenty-four pounds and, by the way, the cake stall's sold out and they raised fourteen pounds and sixty pence.'

'Terrific!' said Tish. 'I'll just squeeze it in at the end of the stencil.'

By Friday, no other group had raised as much as the Action Committee, although the girls who did the sponsored walk came close with forty-one pounds and sixty pence. Whether or not Rebecca and Co. would be the winning group depended very much on the play.

It took place after tea on Friday and made a fitting climax to Charity Week. The weather was kind, as it had been ever since the previous Saturday. Whether it was the beautiful May evening, with a balmy breeze in the air, or sheer curiosity, or both, that drew the crowds, it would be difficult to say. But row upon row of girls sat on the green grass in front of South Terrace waiting eagerly for the play to begin. They had all paid thirty pence for the privilege.

The comedy began with no sign of the players, just the gay, jaunty sound of a violin playing in the trees behind the terrace. Then the figure of Nicola Hodges appeared, dressed as a strolling minstrel, with the instrument tucked beneath her chin, the bow dancing backwards and forwards over the strings. The doors of the Music School were thrown open and out came an assortment of 'woodland folk' dancing comically to the music. The stage was set for fifteen minutes of uproarious fun.

At the end, the audience gave the players a standing ovation and Rebecca clapped as loudly as anyone. Max had taken Roberta's shapeless, wooden play and turned it into something light and magical.

There were loud cheers as the elves and goblins dragged Max out to take a bow. He, in his turn, disappeared into the Music School and reappeared a minute later. He was dragging Roberta Jones forward and holding something behind his back.

'I may have produced the play,' he shouted, 'but here is the person who wrote it, whose brainchild the whole entertainment has been – Bobbie Jones.'

There was polite applause and Roberta stood there blushing. Then a gasp went up as Max produced, from behind his back, a large bouquet of flowers, all wrapped in cellophane. Rebecca had seen the sort in the florist's shop in town, with large price tag to match.

'For all the fun you've given us.' said Max, bowing low.

Everybody entered into the spirit of the thing and cheered loudly. Roberta took the bouquet, clumsily, almost dropping it, her eyes glazed. She couldn't quite believe this was really happening to her. Then the audience, restless now that the fun was over, got to its feet and scattered in all directions. But Roberta just stood there by the little lake, the bouquet clutched to her chest, staring down at her reflection in the water. Was that her, down there? Was it really her?

'Max certainly does everything in style!' exclaimed Sue admiringly, as they walked away. 'And Jenny told me that he's going to treat the whole cast to fizzy drinks at Moffatt's afterwards.'

The celebration was still going on in Moffatt's an hour later. The three friends wanted to go and buy a squash and found they couldn't get in the door. There was a singsong going on, with Max's baritone voice clearly audible.

As they smiled and walked away, Rebecca heard a car screech to a halt on the gravel in front of the tuck shop. They looked back and saw the red sports car that always collected Max from school. The hood was down and as usual the glamorous girl called Katie was at the steering wheel.

She looked furious. As she heard the singing, she did a strange thing. She just put her hand on the car's horn and kept it there. HOONNNNNNKKKKKKKK! Max came running out. She let go of the horn.

'For goodness' sake!' she yelled. 'We're supposed to be taking the Mulliners out for a meal! They're waiting for us!'

'The Mulliners!' Max looked horrified. 'I thought that was next week!'

'Well, it's not. It's now. It's half an hour ago. For heaven's sake get your stuff.'

'It's over in the Staff Room, give me five minutes.'

When Rebecca and Co. went up the steps of old building a little later, Max came flying out, his bag bulging with books to mark, nearly knocking them over. Katie juddered the car over to him and he jumped in.

'Bye, Bobbie!' he shouted as they drove away.

Rebecca saw Roberta Jones standing under the big cedar tree on the far side of the school forecourt. She was still clutching the flowers. On impulse, she walked across to her and glanced at her stricken face.

'Hadn't you better put those in water?' she said kindly. 'Come on, bring them over to Juniper. They'll make a lovely arrangement.'

Roberta cheered up then.

On the way to the boarding house she said, wistfully:

'The play was fun, wasn't it?'

'Terrific fun,' said Sue.

'The whole of Charity Week's been fun!' said Tish suddenly.

It was true. It had been marvellous. So much so that none of them really minded when the Principal announced on Saturday morning that Roberta's had been the winning group. The play had raised sixty pounds. Much more important, a grand total of £292 had been raised for the Animals need Real Kindness Fund.

Somebody went and stole the surfing money.

Rebecca wandered along to the School Office, later Saturday morning, to pick up the cash box. There was thirty pounds in it now and they wanted to collect the rest of the money that was owed and hand in the total to Miss Morgan.

Round about Thursday she had left it as usual with Mrs Devenshire, who had told her to put it on the table by the door.

It wasn't on the table. It wasn't anywhere in the office. It had gone.

NINE
M for Mason

As soon as it became known that the cash box containing the thirty pounds surfing money had been stolen, a sense of outrage ran through Juniper House. It was mean, despicable, unbelievable! Who could have gone into the School Office and calmly lifted it just like that? Who was the creeping, rotten girl responsible?

Mrs Devenshire confirmed that the cash box had been on the table last thing Friday afternoon, before she went home for the weekend. Straight after phoning Mrs Devenshire, Miss Welbeck phoned the police. Two policemen came to the school and asked questions and took notes. Then they drove away again.

'It's horrible, isn't it?' said Joss, serving out the

slices of cold meat at lunch time. There was salad to go with it and potatoes baked in their jackets. 'It must be somebody in the school.'

'I wonder how she's feeling now?' said Rebecca, angrily.

'I don't think the police will catch them,' said Tish. 'I mean, it could be anybody. Anyone at school could have nipped into the School Office. It's never locked or anything. I hate the feeling that it's . . .' she screwed up her nose and glanced round the full dining hall. 'Well, it must be somebody in this hall.'

'I wonder who?' Rebecca paused. 'Maybe it's somebody who's overspent themselves, on sponsorships and things. Just can't find the money and feels panicky. Took the cash box on impulse –'

'It must have been impulse,' agreed Sue. 'A proper thief would have looked to see if the box was locked –'

'Which it wasn't. I'm afraid I never bothered,' interposed Rebecca.

'Then they'd take the money out quickly. Just the large money like the pound coins and the fifty pence pieces, and leave all the two pences and stuff. I mean who'd want to take the box as well! What a risk! It *must* have been impulse.'

'We'll write something for *The J.J.* tomorrow!' said Tish. 'Ask the guilty person to own up and not to be so stupid.'

'And we could do some detective work as well!' suggested Rebecca. 'The thief must have dumped the empty cash box somewhere. We could search for that. And they might have tried to get rid of the small change, in Moffatt's maybe. We could ask Mrs Moffat –'

'Detective work!' Tish nodded vigorously. 'Yes. Action Committee again. I mean, it was us six that raised all that money and it's up to us to try and get it back! Let's start this afternoon!'

'I ought to help, too,' said Joss, listening. 'As I was in the surf. But I'm supervising First Year sprinting this afternoon. Athletics Club. The whole programme's behind. You're behind, too, you know, Rebecca. Sports Day's on Friday week and if you want to be in the 100 and the 200 you've still got to qualify.'

Rebecca was well aware of that. She had cursed there being two wet Saturdays in a row, so that Angela Hessel hadn't come. Athletics Club's activities had been limited to keep-fit training over in the sports centre. She wanted to get out on the track again and had been looking forward to it ever since the fine weather arrived last Sunday. But now –

'Sorry, Joss. I'll have to leave it. I'll make Athletics my option on games afternoons and I'll come next week to Club. But we have to try and do something about this. At least, I do, seeing I was daft enough to leave the cash box there in the first place. If only I hadn't been too lazy to get Miss Morgan to lock it up each time we'd finished collecting . . .'

'Oh, stuff!' said Tish. 'Nobody ever bothers.'

'It's not your fault, Rebecca!' said Elf. She'd finished her jacket potato at last and there was some butter on her chin. 'In fact we could manage without you this afternoon, if it weren't for your fantastic memory.' The detective idea had really captured her imagination. 'Knowing you, you'll remember some vital little detail about somebody's behaviour on Friday –'

'It's okay, Elf. I'm coming this afternoon,' said Rebecca, laughing. 'I've made my mind up about it.'

She did want to go to Athletics Club and get some more coaching from Angela Hessel and run 13.5 seconds – but she wouldn't. They must try and do *something* to find the money. It made her hate the thief all the more.

As it turned out, they didn't find the box, or any clues, that afternoon – although they ransacked the school grounds. Rebecca's photographic memory *didn't* recall any vital little detail. It was all, in short, a waste of time.

Nor did anybody respond to Tish's appeal when it was published in *The Juniper Journal* on Monday. Nor did the police have any success. They soon had to move on to more important crimes.

There was no way of replacing the money, without writing home. Miss Morgan refused to allow them to do that. The cheque just had to go to London thirty pounds smaller than it should have been.

'I feel in my heart that the person with the guilty conscience will own up, sooner or later,' said the junior House Mistress. The theft had distressed her very much for it carried the hallmark of somebody young and impulsive, possibly one of her First Years. 'I think they'll own up, sometime before the end of term. A guilty conscience is a terrible burden to carry around. The best thing you girls can do now is to forget about it.'

But Rebecca and the others from dormitory number six had no intention of forgetting about it. In the fortnight before half-term they went around in a gang more than they'd ever done before. The sponsored surf had brought them close together, but the theft of the money brought them even closer. 'The six detectives', Roberta Jones called them, though not jeeringly, as she might have done once. Roberta was still blossoming and, secretly, she never ceased to marvel at how much time Max seemed to have for her.

The six concentrated their activities on trying to find the missing metal box, which they felt sure the thief must have hidden somewhere in the school buildings or grounds. And although it was like looking for a needle in a haystack, they secretly began to get satisfaction from these activities.

'We've got to persevere,' Tish would say. 'Then sooner or later we'll crack the mystery.'

It was during that fortnight that the question of the new boarding houses first entered Rebecca's mind. She was beginning to despair of maths and dimly in the back of her mind she began to acknowledge that she might have to go into the Beta stream next year. So the question of being in the same boarding house as her friends began to assume importance.

In September all the Second Years would be

leaving Juniper House. They would no longer be juniors, but Third Years and therefore members of the Middle School. The Middle School comprised all the girls in the Third, Fourth and Fifth Years at Trebizon. They were split up equally between five different boarding houses, situated in the school grounds. These were very small units compared with Juniper House, where one hundred and twenty girls lived. Each one housed no more than about thirty-six girls.

'How's it decided which Middle School house we go in?' asked Rebecca.

'Dunno, exactly,' said Tish, who was cleaning her teeth at the time. 'I think we all put our names down at the end of term and they try and keep friends together. But that's years away yet.'

'But they let friends keep together?' asked Rebecca eagerly.

'Pretty sure that's always been the system. It'd better be!'

Rebecca comforted herself with the thought that if by any chance she was put down into III Beta next term, at least she and Sue and Tish would be together other times. How rambling and friendly the Middle School boarding houses looked, with

119

only three dozen girls living in them. She'd heard they had studies, that three or four of you shared together. Mara and Margot and Elf – they must come, too. She was getting fonder of those three all the time. Tish's Action Committee. It was a silly name, but it stuck.

She threw herself into athletics. One afternoon, to her delight, Angela Hessel came to take the group doing athletics, to make up for the two missed Saturdays. She timed Rebecca over the 100 metres sprint.

'13.8 seconds. Get some running spikes by Saturday,' she said. Then added, quite casually: 'They'll make a big difference. You should qualify for Sports Day quite easily.'

Rebecca was overjoyed. She hadn't any money but she got hold of a secondhand pair of running shoes from Miss Willis and asked for them to be put down on her school bill. When she wrote her weekly letter to her parents, she told them what she'd done. She did not, of course, tell them about her secret ambition to run in the County Sports at the end of term, when they would be home from Saudi Arabia. She dreamt of surprising them with that. It was becoming a favourite daydream.

Wearing running spikes at Saturday's Athletics Club meeting she ran the 100 metres in 13.2 seconds, thus fulfilling Angela Hessel's prophecy. She rested for a few minutes and then went straight on to qualify for the 200 metres as well.

'You've got six days until Sports Day,' was all Joss said. 'So you'd better work! You'll have to get below thirteen if you want to be in the first three. Aba can do 12.9 and so can Laura Wilkins in II Beta. Also it's not even worth going through to the Area Sports if you can't get below thirteen seconds.'

'Then I'm going to get below thirteen seconds!' said Rebecca.

Rebecca and Tish trained together. Tish had also qualified for Sports Day – the 800 metres. Sue might have got into the long jump but she had so much music on that she decided to opt out of Athletics. The school orchestra was going to be playing in Exeter over half-term. Any spare time she had, she played tennis.

So the two of them trained like fanatics for six days. They did the special exercises that Angela Hessel recommended, over in the sports centre, as well as athletics every games afternoon. Morning and evening they went jogging, to the far side of Trebizon Bay and back again.

The days were getting hot now but the mornings and evenings were pleasant for running, the sand golden and damp beneath their bare feet.

On the Monday evening, after a particularly sunny day, the heat stayed in the sun quite late. By the time they reached the far side of the bay they were uncomfortably sweaty, even in tee shirts and shorts and bare feet. The sight of the sparkling blue sea and the gulls wheeling above the headland was too much for them. There was nobody around. They broke all the school rules and plunged into the waves just as they were and swam round the headland into Mulberry Cove. They threw themselves on to a flat slab of rock, licked by salt spray, feeling the sun on their backs. Rebecca let her feet trail in the water. She could have lain there forever.

'Voices!' said Tish suddenly, lifting her head.

They crept towards a pile of rocks and peered through them. There, less than twenty yards away, was Max! He, too, was lying outstretched on a slab of rock, in swimming trunks, with his girlfriend, Katie. He was busily marking homework, while the sea water eddied around his feet and threw spray all over the books. He was talking and laughing as he worked and Katie was smoking a cigarette, flicking the ash over the edge of the rock, into the sea.

The girls crept away, plunged into the water and swam back round the headland into Trebizon Bay as fast as they could. They stumbled up on to the sand laughing, supporting each other.

'So that's where he marks our books!'

'I noticed some funny marks on mine the other day!' said Tish. 'He must have got the cover wet!'

'I wish he'd drop mine in the sea!' exclaimed Rebecca.

By the time they'd jogged back to school, right back across the bay, their clothes were almost dry. When Matron saw them in their pyjamas and dressing gowns, drinking cocoa with their hair wet, she presumed they'd just had a shower. 'You should have worn shower caps, you silly girls,' she scolded. 'Hurry up and dry your hair now. It's late.'

One day, before breakfast, they saw Roberta out jogging. She wasn't in Sports Day.

'Making herself beautiful for Max,' whispered Rebecca.

'How's your maths?' Tish asked suddenly.

'Oh, Tish, don't let's talk about maths. It's

glorious this morning – I'm going to sprint!'

Rebecca streaked away across the sand, her fair hair flowing out behind her like a windsock, straight up a sand dune and on to the top. She threw her arms up and gazed up at the sky. 'Just glorious!'

However, when Rebecca's form-mistress, Miss Heath, got hold of her on Friday morning and said 'Let's talk about your maths', there was no such escape. The girls would be breaking up for half-term at the end of the afternoon, after Sports Day, and Miss Heath was anxious to speak to Rebecca.

'I've been looking at your marks so far this term,' she said. 'They're abominable. It would be a pity for a girl of your intelligence to have to go into III Beta next term, but that's what's going to happen, Rebecca, if you don't pull your socks up.'

'Threats!' said Sue, at morning break. 'Just threats!'

'I'm not so sure,' said Rebecca, uncomfortably.

Mara's news was the reverse of Rebecca's. She was elated because Mrs Beal, her form-mistress, had taken her and another girl called Jane Bowen on one side after the geography lesson.

'She as good as said that Jane Bowen and I'll go up into the Alpha class in September, just as long as our exam marks are as good as our term work!'

'Oh, Mara!' Elf hugged her. 'Good. Good!'

'Swot!' teased Tish.

'Once we're all together, I'll never swot again!' promised Mara. 'I just hate being the odd one out.'

'It'll be perfect, us all being together,' said Sue.

'I know,' nodded Tish. But she glanced across at Rebecca, with a slightly worried expression on her face.

Rebecca was downcast by Miss Heath's words. Sue refused to believe it and Tish was unsure. But Rebecca knew it had to be faced; she might go down. Her parents would be disappointed if that happened. But it was no use, she just couldn't get on with Max's way of teaching. If only that Mrs Shaw person had been able to come this term!

She was further downcast when all the parents started arriving for Sports Day, straight after lunch. She wished hers were in England. Sue's weren't coming, either, because none of the school orchestra would be going home for half-term. Tish's parents were the next best thing. They knew Sue well, but they'd never met Rebecca before. They took both girls under their wing.

'So this is Rebecca!' said Doctor Anderson, who

had a lovely crinkled-up face. 'Here, have some chocolate. Give you energy.'

'You said she was brainy, Tish,' came a boy's voice, just behind Rebecca. 'You never told us she looked quite normal.'

Rebecca turned round and found herself shaking hands with a tall, strong-looking boy who had a big laughing mouth, just like Tish's, and the same humorous brown eyes.

'I'm not brainy,' Rebecca said quickly, hating herself for blushing.

'This is my brother, Robbie,' said Tish. 'It's his half-term, too. My parents have just picked him up.' His own boarding school, Garth College, was just on the other side of town. A lot of Trebizon girls seemed to have brothers there.

'You two had better win,' said Robbie, 'seeing we've come to watch.'

'The tea's quite good,' riposted Rebecca.

But she suddenly felt cheerful again. She had to win something this afternoon! If she could get into the County Sports at the end of term, that would make up to her parents for anything else! It suddenly seemed the most important thing in the world.

The day was sunny again and the ground was

firm. There was almost no breeze. Her first race – the 100 metres junior sprint – was nearly due. There were crowds of girls and parents lining the running track, a lot of them bunched up by the finishing line. She'd pretend her parents were there, amongst them. She'd pretend it was the County Sports.

The starting pistol cracked. They were off first time!

Rebecca knew she'd started well. She was in the first four and the pace was terrific. Straight all the way! No bends! She hurtled along and at the halfway point she could see Laura Wilkins to her left and Aba Amori to her right, the rest of the field drumming along behind the three of them. There was a lot of cheering and noise. Rebecca was conscious of only one thing now, the dominating presence of the Nigerian girl at her right shoulder – the long dark legs striking out, head, neck and shoulders forward.

The tape was coming up and Rebecca knew that she must accelerate or Aba would leave her for dead. For two electrifying seconds they fought it out, shoulder to shoulder. 'REBECK!' that was Tish's voice. '*Come on Rebecca!*' – her brother's! Rebecca edged in front and hurled herself forward at the tape. She felt it touch her and she ran on through it, arms raised, gasping for air.

She'd won!

'12.7 seconds, Rebecca. Very well done!' said Miss Willis, soon after. Joanne Hissup herself came and threw an arm round her shoulders.

'You're a County prospect, Rebecca!' she said in delight.

Aba hugged her sportingly. Joss Vining, Tish, Sue –

they were all converging! 'Marvellous!' said Joss.

'Whatever happens in the 200, you've got through to the Area Sports!' exclaimed Tish. 'Oh, gosh, it's my race soon!'

Rebecca felt elated. If only her parents could have seen her run! Funnily enough, she would have liked Max to have seen her, too. She'd have liked him to see that there was *something* she was good at. But Max had vanished. Roberta Jones had been looking all over for him, to introduce her parents, until Debbie Rickard had informed her that the red sports car had carried him away directly after morning lessons.

Tish won the junior 800 metres and she, too, qualified for the Area Sports. Aba and Laura also qualified. They got their revenge in the 200 metres by beating Rebecca into third place. That didn't dampen Rebecca's spirits in the least. Now she knew that she must concentrate all her efforts on the 100 metres. She would work and work at it between now and the Area Sports – the last barrier between her and the County Sports, when her parents would be home!

There was a party atmosphere that afternoon, not least because the senior girls had finished their big exams the very same morning.

Tea was set out on the big terrace in front of the dining hall, overlooking the quadrangle gardens. It was eaten and enjoyed in brilliant sunshine. The dainty sandwiches, sausage rolls and delicious pastries were, by amazing sleight of hand, conjured from the school kitchens – the same place from which stews and bean bakes and other stolid fare so often emanated.

'Why do the cooks hide their light under a bushel?' asked Rebecca, sinking her teeth into a third chocolate eclair.

'It's just to impress visitors,' said Tish.

'Then I'm impressed,' said Robbie, through a mouthful of gateau.

'Have a happy half-term!' said Pippa Fellowes-Walker later.

'I shall!' replied Rebecca.

But when she arrived at her grandmother's the next day and was shown the circular letter, all her happiness evaporated.

Rebecca's grandmother, who was her guardian while her parents were abroad, had received the notice earlier in the week. She showed it to Rebecca on the Saturday evening, quite casually:

ARRANGEMENTS FOR TRANSFER OF SECOND YEAR
GIRLS TO NEW BOARDING HOUSES IN SEPTEMBER.

*Your daughter will be leaving the junior boarding
house at the end of this term, having completed her
first two years at Trebizon. She will be transferred
to one of five Middle School boarding houses, where
she will remain for her next three years. These are
smaller units with a family atmosphere where girls
are allowed a greater degree of freedom than in
Juniper House.*

*We have tried in the past to accommodate the
wishes of girls and their parents in the matter of
choice of boarding house, but we have found this
system to be unworkable because some houses are
always oversubscribed. We have, therefore, decided
to allocate the girls to the five boarding houses in
groups of twelve, taken in strict alphabetical order
down through the three streams as follows:*

Girls 1–12 (III Alpha): COURT HOUSE

Girls 13–18 (III Alpha) and 1–6 (III Beta):
NORRIS HOUSE

Girls 7–18 (III Beta): STERNDALE HOUSE

Girls 19–21 (III Beta) and 1–9 (III Gamma):
TAVISTOCK HOUSE

Girls 10–21 (III Gamma): CHAMBERS HOUSE

These numbers are based on present streaming and do not allow for end-of-term adjustments. The general principle is clear: to allow most girls to be with a group from their own form in their new boarding house. Arrangements will also be made for sisters to remain together. House lists will be posted up at school after Summer Exams when Third Year streaming has been finalised.

Madeleine Welbeck, *Principal*

Rebecca read the notice through three times.

'What's the matter, Rebecca?'

'Er – nothing, Gran.'

She got out a pencil from the jar on the kitchen dresser and wrote down the names of the girls in her form – in alphabetical order:

Aba Amori, Tish Anderson, Mary Bron, Jenny Brook-Hayes, Sally Elphinstone, Ann Ferguson, Anne Finch, Roberta Jones, Elizabeth Kendall, Margot Lawrence, Rebecca Mason, Sue Murdoch, Ruth Nathan, Sarah Nathan, Debbie Rickard, Judy Sharp, Joanna Thompson, Joss Vining.

She sectioned off the first twelve names in II Alpha

by putting a stroke after Sue's name. If the whole form went up to III Alpha, just as it stood, she and Sue would go into Court House with Tish and Margot and Elf – they'd all be together, with the exception of Mara.

But that wasn't going to happen! Jane and Mara were coming up to III Alpha, it was as good as settled. Jane Bowen and Mara Leonodis. So they would be in the first twelve! They'd go into Court House with Tish and the others, while Rebecca and Sue would go into Norris House.

That was bad enough, but there was something infinitely worse.

Rebecca might go into III Beta!

Would she still then go into Norris House with Sue? The names of present Beta form girls ran through her mind . . . *Susan Carter, Elizabeth Fichumi, Jane Ford, Helena King, Penny Leason, Rachel Lee*. There were at least six before Mason! She wouldn't go into Norris House with Sue. She'd go into Sterndale House, on her own.

It was bad enough for Sue, but at least she'd be seeing Tish and the others in lessons every day. If Rebecca went into the Beta stream next term she'd be separated from the others all the time! The very name Sterndale House sounded hateful – like a prison!

The letter 'M' was even more hateful – M for Mason – and maths.

She worried about it all weekend. When she got back to school after half-term, the crowd in dormitory six could talk of nothing else. It was like trying to do a difficult crossword puzzle, working out all the possible combinations – who might go up, who might go down – who had a sister – who would go into which house. Rebecca couldn't bring herself to join in. Then Sue said something which proved to be the last straw.

'Cheer up, Rebecca. It's maddening, I know. But Court and Norris are right next door to each other – not like Sterndale or somewhere, stuck away on its own. And we'll all be together for lessons.'

'I used to think you were bright!' snapped Rebecca, miserably. She stalked off. 'I'm going to the library.'

Tish and Sue followed her there, two minutes later, and found her in floods of tears.

TEN
The House Lists Go Up

'I'm sorry, Sue,' sniffed Rebecca, 'but it was just too much when you said that. I just *know* I'll be going into Beta and that means I *will* end up in Sterndale, stuck away on my own . . .'

She was crying like a baby and she couldn't stop it! It was humiliating. Tish and Sue put their arms around her waist and walked her over to the window. Pippa Fellowes-Walker was on library duty, sorting out some books on a shelf, looking their way.

'Ssssh! Pippa'll chuck us out of the library,' soothed Tish.

'This idea you've got! About going into Beta! It's really stupid!' said Sue stubbornly.

'My marks!' gulped Rebecca. 'The highest I've had in maths all term is seven out of twenty! You should see my book!'

'That's only because Max doesn't bother with anyone, except Robert!' said Tish. 'Miss Gates won't worry about your term's work – she doesn't like him! As long as you can scrape together about forty-five per cent in the exam, they won't dream of putting you down –'

'Or even forty,' said Sue triumphantly, glad that Tish seemed to agree with her. 'Because you're okay at everything else!'

'How am I going to do that?' asked Rebecca

helplessly. She'd stopped crying now She just felt fatalistic. She was never, never going to be any good at maths, no matter how hard she tried!

'Because we're going to help you, silly,' said Tish.

'You can't!' said Rebecca, shocked. Then she realised what Tish meant.

They all started laughing. Pippa was standing right behind them and she was laughing, too. For the first time, Rebecca began to feel better.

'I don't think anyone can help you in the exam itself!' said Pippa. 'But if you're going to have some maths coaching, it'd be better from somebody older. I've finished my big exams, so I could do it. I'll have to ask Miss Gates, of course.'

'You!' exclaimed Rebecca. Had she heard right? 'Do you mean it?'

'Of course I mean it! Now shut up making such a noise in here, you three, and go and make a noise somewhere else.'

'Yes, that girl Mason's got a lot of ground to make up,' said Miss Gates, when Pippa came to see her. 'If I weren't so busy with the GCSE Year, I'd try and take her in hand myself. Of course, Dennis Maxwell should do it really. The trouble with that young man,' she said acidly, 'is that as soon as the afternoon bell goes he's out of the front door like a scalded cat. Not that I should be discussing that with you.'

Pippa hid a smile. The friction between Miss Gates and the temporary maths master had reached almost legendary proportions. It was early June and Max spent every spare moment swimming and sunbathing in Mulberry Cove. His tan won admiration from the girls, but further hostility from Miss Gates.

'Now I'm convinced of it!' she told Miss Welbeck. 'He may have a brilliant brain, but he's just a layabout like all the rest who come down here for the summer. He's taken this job to get some stamps on his card! He's probably counting the days to the end of term, when he'll be able to draw unemployment benefit and have a jolly good time of it, like all the rest of them. I don't know what you see in him, Madeleine.'

'He has splendid references, Evelyn.'

'Written by his Cambridge friends, I daresay!'

'One or two girls have come along remarkably under him. Roberta Jones, for instance.'

'Roberta Jones!' Snort! 'I'll believe that when I

see her exam result.'

Having written Max off as a lost cause, Miss Gates readily agreed to the prefect's suggestion.

'It's very kind of you, Pippa. It might give Miss Hort a few less pieces to pick up when the new academic year arrives and Dennis Maxwell is no longer with us.'

Miss Hort was in charge of maths in the Middle School.

The month of June was glorious. The long, hot summer that Tish had hopefully predicted at the beginning of term was really coming to pass. Most evenings Rebecca had to go and water her plants in the kitchen garden, or they'd have died. She enjoyed that peaceful task at the end of the busy days, when the heat had gone out of the sun. She could watch the martins darting in and out of their nests under the eaves of the old stables, which overlooked the big walled garden.

She was happy again now. Pippa was coaching her and maths had lost some of their mystery – like the time Tish had explained to her about the binary system. It was all very hard work, but things were beginning to fall into place.

The days were too crowded and busy to think

about her parents, but she would think about them those evenings when the garden was heavy with summer scents and the spraying water made a cool sound. They were coming back to England soon for their summer leave! If she won her race in the Area Sports, at the beginning of July, she'd write and tell them that they could come and see her run in the County Sports, on July fifteenth. They'd be home by then!

It was a bit of a daydream, really.

Rebecca was getting nowhere near as much athletics training as she needed. In the second half of term, games lessons were taken up with swimming in the sea and surfing and tennis. Rebecca was starting to love tennis. The afternoons spent in the sea were sheer paradise. But with Sports Day over, athletics no longer figured in the official timetable. Athletics Club, training sessions in the gym, matches with other schools – all these took place out of school hours. Rebecca was offered a place in the athletics team and she had to turn it down. With all the extra maths, she simply didn't have the time. She went jogging with Tish most mornings before breakfast and hoped that would be enough.

'It won't be!' Miss Willis told her, rather sharply.

'You need to run against some good competition before the Area Sports. But if you can't come to training sessions and fixtures then you can't, I suppose.'

Rebecca worked hard, all through June. Pippa was patient and explained things well, going over the groundwork that Rebecca had missed in the First Year. The maths syllabus at her London school had been completely different. She began to enjoy maths lessons more, now that she could sometimes understand what Max was talking about. Slowly her marks began to improve. She worked hard revising for the other exams, too. A few evenings the others would drag her away from her books to go surf-riding. Mara would come, too, though she would sometimes bring her school books down to the beach, as she couldn't surf. She was working at least as hard as Rebecca, leaving nothing to chance.

They always came back to Juniper House starving hungry and raided the kitchen and talked and laughed long after lights out.

Those evenings were such fun that it made Rebecca sad to think that the six of them could never be in the same boarding house again, let alone in the same dormitory. The best she could hope for was to be with them in III Alpha next year and go into Norris House with Sue. But with Tish, in particular, in a different house, nothing would be quite the same again. Rebecca knew that Sue felt the same way, although they never spoke about it.

The June roses in the quadrangle gardens began to wilt; the days got still hotter. Suddenly it was the first week of July – Summer Exams week. Exams lasted from Monday to Friday and the Area Sports meeting was on the Saturday.

For five days the girls of II Alpha bent their heads over examination papers, in a room silent except for the scratching of cartridge pens and the buzzing of flies. The little room, high up in old building, seemed to get hotter and stuffier each day. Rebecca would gaze out at the bright sky and the little scudding clouds, thinking with longing of the blue waters of Trebizon Bay. But she was glad that she'd worked for the exams. On the whole, they didn't seem too bad.

Her greatest sense of relief came with the last exam, on Friday. It was the maths paper. It covered two years' work and lasted two and a half hours. As she worked her way through the questions, Rebecca felt grateful to Pippa. She was on familiar ground with a lot of the problems that had been set, though there were some she couldn't do. Tish, Sue, Margot and Elf crowded round her afterwards, eager to know how she'd got on.

'I think –' Rebecca swallowed hard. She didn't want to tempt providence. 'I *think* I may have passed.'

'If *you* think so, then you must have done!' said Tish jubilantly.

'Look at Robert's long face!' whispered Elf. 'I don't think she's done very well, in spite of all the help she's had from Max.'

'What about Mary Bron then – and Joanna – they both looked as though they could burst into tears!' said Margot, as the five came out of the form room in a knot. 'Let's go and see how Mara's got on!'

Mara had got on famously.

That was the best evening Rebecca could remember. About twenty of them went swimming and surfing and finished up with a barbecue on the beach: an end-of-exams celebration, with Miss Morgan's permission.

They cooked sausages on the fire and watched a magnificent sunset over the sea. It was getting late.

'Come on, Becky,' said Tish. 'We'd better go

now. We've got to run tomorrow, this lot haven't!'

'Coming!' said Rebecca. She could hear the distant sound of the waves and her face was glowing in the firelight. She had to drag herself away. She wanted the party to go on for ever because she felt as though she had a lot to celebrate. Afterwards, she wondered what could have made her feel that way.

Probably because she hadn't done enough training, Rebecca flopped at the Area Sports. She ran the 100 metres junior sprint in 13.2 seconds and there were five girls ahead of her. So she didn't qualify for the County Sports.

Tish fared better, coming second in the 800 metres, and Aba Amori actually won the 200 metres, which was her best distance. Joanna Hissup cleared 1.74 metres to win the senior high jump event with ease and Joss Vining won the junior long jump.

'We've done pretty well as a school,' said Tish, on the long minibus journey back to Trebizon. Miss Willis was driving. 'But it's a shame about you.'

'I'm furious with myself,' said Rebecca. A cloud of depression was settling over her. 'I never told you, did I, but my parents will be back here by July fifteenth – you know, the County Sports . . .' Her voice trailed away. 'I'd been hoping all along . . .'

She lapsed into silence and Tish let her brood. But after a while Tish said: 'There's always next year. Much better to pass the maths exam this year.' Rebecca cheered up a little after that.

But it seemed that her confidence was ill-founded.

When Max read out the results of the maths exam the following Wednesday, they were not, admittedly, very brilliant. Only three girls, Tish and Anne Finch and Joss Vining, had got over seventy per cent. Nevertheless, the rest of the form had all scraped above fifty per cent – including Roberta Jones – with the exception of four girls. Debbie Rickard had forty-five per cent, Joanna Thompson had forty-one per cent, Mary Bron had thirty-two per cent and last of all came Rebecca with twenty-eight per cent.

Twenty-eight per cent! At first Rebecca's mind simply couldn't take it in. She thought she must have misheard. But one look at Sue's face was enough. Sue had never been seriously worried about Rebecca. But she was now. In fact she was gaping at her in amazement, her jaw sagging. Tish was aghast.

The rest of the lesson passed in a blur for Rebecca. As the bell went, they started to crowd round her, to sympathise – not just her friends but people like Anne Finch and the Nathan twins. They all knew how hard she'd worked. Even Roberta Jones was coming over. She was in a daze for a different reason. She'd got sixty-one per cent in the exam and still couldn't quite believe it.

Rebecca couldn't stand sympathy from anybody, not even her best friends. What point was there in talking about it? There was nothing more to say! She'd known all along she would never be any good at maths! Whatever had made her think otherwise? The whole thing had been an illusion!

She shot away out of the form room and down the stairs. It was morning break and she went to find Pippa, who was out in the grounds, sketching.

'I've let you down,' she said, flatly. 'I got twenty-eight per cent and came bottom.'

'Rebecca!' The prefect stared at her. 'I don't believe it.'

'It's true.'

'Oh.' Pippa was really surprised. 'Bottom! After all that slogging! And you seemed to be getting on so well!' She stood up and put an arm round Rebecca's shoulders. 'Were you nervous?'

'Not particularly. I'm not good at maths, that's all.'

146

'No, Rebecca! It's not that.' Pippa searched for an explanation. 'I suppose,' she said, becoming resigned, 'that a month just wasn't long enough. You'll catch up in the end.'

'But I'll have to go into III Beta now,' said Rebecca, trying very hard not to cry.

'Perhaps,' said Pippa. 'I know it's hard to take, but maths is so important and you've got to learn it. It's no use going faster than you can cope with. Wait and see what happens.'

She watched Rebecca walk away, very nearly in tears herself. What a shame! She'd done her best to help, but it hadn't made any difference. She was surprised, all the same. She would tell Miss Gates how surprised she was.

The House Lists were posted up on the noticeboards, the last weekend of term. The school would break up the following Thursday. Knowing the lists were going to be put up, Rebecca could hardly eat any lunch on Saturday, though Elf tried to coax her, telling her how delicious the cold savoury pie was. Tish and Sue said nothing. They weren't very hungry themselves. Sue hated herself for never having taken Rebecca's fears seriously, right through the term.

Now, with Rebecca and the others, she feared the worst.

On the next dinner table, Roberta Jones was on tenterhooks.

'I'll die if I'm not put in III Beta,' she announced.

'III Beta?' asked Mara in amazement. It was common knowledge by now that Roberta had been trying hard all term, especially with maths, in order to stay in the Alpha stream.

Roberta and Debbie Rickard exchanged meaningful looks.

Previously, in spite of frequent overtures from Debbie, the ungainly Roberta had been far too lacking in confidence herself to go around with someone as unpopular as Debbie Rickard. She had just formed a trio with the quiet Nathan twins. Not any longer. Max, and the play, had changed so much! As Roberta had blossomed she'd taken Debbie under her wing, with the result that Debbie Rickard had become a much nicer person, especially after winning a lot of praise for her performance in the play. Now Roberta had what she'd always wanted, a best friend of her own.

'If I stay in the Alpha form I'll go in Court House,' said Roberta, making a face. 'I want to go in Norris!

Debbie and me and the twins have just worked it all out. If I go into III Beta we can all be in Norris together!'

'But you'd be in a different form from them –' began Mara.

'Who minds about that!' said Roberta stolidly. 'You can't have any fun in lessons. They've got studies for four in Norris and we'd all share one – we're planning to start a middle school drama group –'

'What about your parents?' asked Laura Wilkins. 'They'd mind!'

'No they wouldn't!' said Roberta. 'I thought they would but Daddy wrote to me during exams and told me not to worry. He said there's a lot more to life than having your head in books – and things like writing the play and raising the most money were actually more important.'

'He's got something there,' nodded Mara. She'd long ago decided that she'd done enough swotting this term to last an entire lifetime. Just as long as she could be with the others now!

So when the House Lists went up, a cry of disappointment came from Roberta. She was going to be in III Alpha – and Court House.

'It's not fair!' She went storming off. 'I'm going to find Gatesy! I'm going to tell her that maths exam was just a fluke!'

There was a lot of laughter. It was such an amazing turnabout.

Rebecca and her friends weren't laughing at the House Lists. They were looking at them leadenly.

It could have been wonderful. Mara had won her place in III Alpha and was down to be in Court House with Tish and Margot and Elf – and Sue as well!

Sue couldn't quite believe her eyes. She wasn't going to be in Norris House on her own, after all. Mary Bron had been put down to III Beta and placed in Norris House, which meant that Sue just scraped into Court House with the others, as number twelve!

It wasn't wonderful, though. For there was Rebecca, down in III Beta, in the Sterndale House group – all on her own. It spoilt everything.

'Oh, Rebecca,' whispered Mara.

Her father, the shipowner, had sent a magnificent iced cake to school for them all. It was in a box in Miss Morgan's office and there, as far as Mara was concerned, it could stay.

ELEVEN
The Cash Box Comes Back

On Saturday afternoon, instead of getting the cake, the six of them wandered around the school grounds trying to think of something to do. The fact that Rebecca was going to be separated from the rest of them, next term, just didn't bear thinking about. Nobody was willing to refer to it.

Rebecca was relieved about that. She just wanted to shut it out of her mind now. But it wouldn't go away. It hung silently in the air.

'Shall we go surfing?' suggested Margot. 'Harry's on duty.'

Tish looked up at the sky and made a face. For the first time in weeks the weather looked threatening. The clouds were a navy-blue colour over Trebizon Bay. The others looked up, too.

'No,' sighed Margot. 'Don't let's.'

'What about badminton?' said Sue, trying to sound bright.

Thumbs down to badminton.

They mooched along the paths that led to the Hilary, kicking bits of gravel as they went, and then stood for a while by the little lake. Rebecca tried to make some stones skim on the water, but they wouldn't. Tish took pot shots at a clump of water weed in the middle and missed.

'We've got to do *The J.J.* this weekend,' she said suddenly.'

'It's funny to think it's our Farewell Issue.'

It was Mara's father who had given the little duplicator to Juniper House but next term, when they moved on to the Middle School boarding houses, they'd be leaving it behind. *The Juniper Journal*, which Tish and Mara had started in Rebecca's first term, would carry on under different editors.

'Our last issue,' said Rebecca.

'We must try and make it good!' said Tish quickly, anxious not to strike a down-note. 'Some really crazy "Did-You-Knows?", for a start.'

'Can't think of any,' replied Rebecca, listlessly.

They wandered on.

'We never did find out who took the surfing money,' said Elf.

'We never even found a single clue!' added Sue. 'And we swore we'd solve the mystery before the end of term!'

'Let's search the grounds again!' said Tish resolutely.

'Good idea!' agreed Rebecca. 'Let's really search! She *must* have dumped the cash box somewhere – the thief – she wouldn't dare keep it in school.' They'd been over this so often before. But now Rebecca felt angry, all over again. 'We swore we'd never give up.'

They searched in some really weird places for they had long ago exhausted the more obvious ones. Rebecca climbed the big cedar tree by the main school forecourt and looked along the huge, spreading branches. There was no sign of the cash box, but she was pleased to have something active to do – and at least it was something worthwhile. They even searched St Mary's, the little church that was set in a secluded, tree-shaded corner of the school grounds and was never kept locked. Rebecca felt slightly sacrilegious as she and Sue crawled along on hands and knees, looking under the pews, while Tish and Margot and Mara hunted in the bell tower and Elf kept guard. But, as always, they drew a blank.

They were halfway back to school when a livid scar of lightning lit up the sky; then came a great crash of thunder and the heavens opened. They went running into the sports centre for shelter, at just the same time as Roberta Jones, who came running in on her way back from Willoughby House. She'd heard Miss Gates was over there, giving a Lower Sixth girl a maths tutorial. She'd waited a whole hour, determined to catch the senior mistress when she came out, for she was still upset about the House Lists. Her patience had been rewarded.

'What on earth did Gatesy say?' asked Tish, curiously.

'She listened to me very carefully,' said Roberta. Her hair was wet and she looked bedraggled. 'She asked me a whole lot of questions, she even asked me the name of my last school and whether Max actually taught me there. I can't see what that's got to do with it, mind you. But the main point is,' Roberta's eyes were bright with hope, 'I think maybe I've convinced her that I'm not all that good at maths and would do better in the Beta stream.

She's taking a special interest in my case.'

'Poor old Robert!' said Tish, as the large girl went off to find a hairdryer in the changing rooms. 'Who's she kidding?'

'Was Miss Gates really as polite as all that?' wondered Mara.

'Yes, she was probably stunned,' said Sue.

Rebecca said nothing, for she was experiencing a deep pang of bitterness. If only she and Roberta could change places! Life just wasn't fair.

The others looked at her and knew exactly what she must be thinking.

'Come on, the rain's easing off a bit,' said Elf. 'Let's dash back to Juniper. Looks as though it's going to be wet all afternoon.'

They ran back to the junior boarding house and went along to the Hobbies Room.

'Let's start to think what we're going to put in the Farewell Issue of *The J.J.*,' said Tish. 'We'll get hold of Susannah.'

'We haven't solved the mystery then,' sighed Mara.

'It's sickening!' Rebecca burst out. 'We've tried so hard. It's sickening to think of the thirty pounds lining somebody's pockets when it could be helping those animals.'

'Miss Morgan said the person would own up before the end of term,' remembered Elf. 'Well, they'd better get a move on, they've only got till Thursday.'

'That's right,' said Rebecca, thinking how upset Miss Morgan had been. 'She said a guilty conscience's a terrible burden to carry around! Well, at this rate, the person concerned's going to have a ton weight on their shoulders all the summer holidays – for the rest of their life, maybe!'

'Got it!' exclaimed Tish. '*The J.J.!*'

'*The J.J.?*'

'*That's* what we must do. One last appeal to the guilty person. Not just a couple of lines, like we did before. We'll make it the main story, pulling no punches, a full-blooded appeal, saying just what thirty pounds can do for an animal that's ill and in pain –'

'Rebecca must write it!' said Sue, clapping her hands. 'You remember, Rebecca, that marvellous piece you wrote before Charity Week –'

'Who else!' said Tish. Her black curls were full of bounce, she was waving her arms around like the editor of an important daily newspaper instead of a five-pence news-sheet. 'Just supposing it works – what a scoop for *The J.J.*! We'll go out on a high! *Will* you write it, Rebeck?'

'I'll try!' said Rebecca eagerly.

'Don't let's ask the guilty person to own up,' said Mara realistically. 'That would be hoping for too much. Let's appeal to them to return the cash box, with the thirty pounds in it, anonymously.'

'Good idea!'

'Where can we ask them to leave it?'

'The church!' said Rebecca. 'Just outside in the porch. No one goes there much during the week. The girl who took the money – she can sneak over there, through the trees – no one will see her. We'll tell her she can leave it there, any time, and we'll check every morning before breakfast to see if it's come back.'

'Tell her she's only got till Thursday! Tell her time is running out!' said Margot.

'I think I'll go to the library right now,' said Rebecca, 'and scribble down a few sentences.' There was an intent look in her eyes. 'It's taking shape, what to say. Thanks, Margot, I think I can see how it should go . . .'

'Go on then!' Tish pushed Rebecca towards

the door, excitedly. 'Quick, before you lose your inspiration! Try and make it the best thing you've ever written.'

'You bet!' thought Rebecca. 'I want to go out on a high, too.'

The piece that Rebecca wrote won much praise. Tish gave it a simple, direct headline: 'Please Get Rid of Your Guilty Conscience, Whoever You Are. This is Your Last Chance.' The words that followed were also simple and direct – and very moving.

The J.J. sold round the school on Monday rather faster than usual. When Miss Morgan delivered the regular order of twenty-four copies to the Staff Room, she did so with pride.

'I've had my ups and downs with them,' she told Mrs Dalzeil, 'but on the whole I think this is the best lot of Second Years I've ever had.'

Rebecca and Co. kept wondering on Monday if *The J.J.* would have any effect on the thief.

'Just think,' said Elf, 'the cash box might be there in the morning.'

'I don't think so,' said Sue. 'That would be too soon. The person needs time to think about it. But as Thursday gets nearer – and it's their last chance to do something before the summer holidays – then maybe it'll really hit them hard. What Rebecca's written.'

'I don't think anything'll happen for a day or two,' agreed Tish.

But they were both wrong.

Late on Monday evening, in the long shadows, a figure dodged through the trees until the church came in sight. St Mary's looked silent and deserted. The only movement came from a bat, swooping down and round in the still night air, making a series of configurations before it darted back into the bell tower.

The figure waited and waited until, convinced that the coast was clear, it crept forward through the little wicket gate and up the path to the church. The huge oak door into the dark porch swung open easily to the touch. The figure entered, took the metal cash box out of a carrier bag and deposited it carefully on the porch seat. Then the person backed out, pulled the porch door shut, turned and walked away up the path.

'Stop!' said a voice.

The culprit stood stock still, then slowly turned. The porch door had opened again and a sepulchral grey-haired figure stood there, holding the cash box. Miss Gates had been sitting inside the church since sunset, waiting and listening.

'I telephoned Greencourt this morning,' she said in hollow tones, her voice echoing in the porch. 'I suggest we leave the cash box here overnight, so the girls can find it in the morning. I shall make an appointment for us both to see Miss Welbeck after Assembly, if that's convenient.'

'Damn,' said Max.

TWELVE
Sorting out Max

The six crept out of the dormitory early, while Jenny and Joanna were still fast asleep, and ran across the school grounds to St Mary's church.

Tish was the first to open the door.

'It's there!' she shrieked.

They all crowded into the porch, blinking in the darkness as they came in from the early morning sun. They stared at the cash box in disbelief. Then they pushed Rebecca forward.

'Go on, Rebecca! You open it!'

Her fingers were shaking as she opened the lid and took out thirty pound coins and counted them. There was a square of paper lying at the bottom of the box. The others crushed round her as she took it out.

'What's it say?'

There was just one word written on the slip of paper, in block capitals:

SORRY

'Oh,' gasped Rebecca. 'Isn't it marvellous?'

She'd sent out a message to somebody unknown, written from the heart – and the message had got through! The person had responded! Responded at once! It was a very special moment for Rebecca.

They ran all the way back to school with the cash box, jubilant.

'I wonder who it was?' said Margot.

'I don't suppose we'll ever know,' said Sue.

'Who cares!' said Rebecca, in awe. 'We've got the money back. We can send it to the Fund now. They've given the money back – and they're sorry! That's all that matters!'

The news spread round the school. By the time Rebecca and Co. went into the dining hall at breakfast time, just about everybody knew. They were greeted by cheers and banging cutlery. Miss Morgan, on duty, hurried over to them as they took their places.

'Well done, all of you!' she said. 'Especially you, Rebecca.'

First lesson was maths and Max didn't turn up. Jacquinda Meredith, the senior prefect, came into the form room to keep order until he arrived.

'How long will he be?' asked Roberta.

'Not very long, now,' replied Jacquinda. 'He had to go and see Miss Welbeck and Miss Gates. They asked to see your exam papers, so he's had to go home and fetch them, but he won't be long.'

A faint stir of interest ran through the room, but Rebecca wasn't even listening. Before the lesson began she'd started reading a P. G. Wodehouse under the desk and was now deeply engrossed.

Roberta Jones nudged Debbie Rickard, hard. Margot had changed places with Roberta some time ago, so that those two could sit next to each other in class.

'I bet it's to do with me!' Roberta whispered. 'I said Miss Gates was going to take a special interest in my case.'

For once she was right.

What was taking place in the Principal's study had quite a lot to do with Roberta, though not exactly in the way she imagined, and Miss Gates had indeed taken a special interest in her case.

After catching Max at the church the night before,

she'd gone over to Miss Welbeck's house and had a word with her. So when Max entered the Principal's study, immediately after morning Assembly, there was an icy reception waiting for him. Both women were seated, with their arms folded, not looking in the least friendly.

'Sit down, Dennis,' said Miss Welbeck, nodding towards a chair.

Max threw himself down in the chair, looking rather hangdog. He crossed his knees and flicked some dust off his elegant trousers. Then he smoothed down his dark hair nervously.

'I'm afraid I'm hopeless with money,' he launched forth. 'I was in a dreadful hole that Friday evening when I shoved the cash box in my brief case. I was supposed to be taking some terribly smart friends of Katie's out for a meal, and I'd spent my last quids buying some flowers for Bobbie Jones and having a bit of a party for the rest of the kids . . .'

'I'm sure a member of staff could have given you a loan,' said Miss Welbeck coldly. 'Did that not occur to you?'

'I couldn't find anybody – and Katie was in a furious temper because we were late and –' Max spread his hands out. 'What else could I do? Of course, I had every intention of paying it back. I was going to send an anonymous donation to those animal people in London.'

'And did you?' inquired Miss Gates.

'Well, no. I was just getting round to thinking about it, when I saw what those kids had written in the news-sheet yesterday. I'd no idea they were still brooding about it! So I thought I'd give them a nice surprise. Do what they suggested and take the money over to the church. I didn't think anyone would be spying on me!' he added, quite indignantly.

There was silence for a few moments. It was broken by Miss Welbeck.

'It was a pity there was nobody to jog your memory in similar fashion at Greencourt. Were you going to pay back the money there? The money for the school trip to France, that had been entrusted to your care? And if you were, why did you say it had been stolen from your flat when in fact you'd spent it on a new car?'

Max looked at Miss Welbeck from under his dark lashes and then flicked some more dust from his trouser leg. He was not deeply disturbed.

'I did pay it back, in time. Of course, it was rather a large sum. But I found some way of paying it back. I had the most deadly run of bad luck at Greencourt. I crashed the car and it wasn't insured and I had to have some transport in a hurry – I only borrowed the money.'

'You were very lucky not to go to prison,' said Miss Gates, who had telephoned the headmistress of Greencourt first thing on Monday morning and got the full story from her. 'It was all hushed up.'

'Was it? I wasn't sure. I left the district rather soon after that.'

'Neither the children nor their parents were ever told why you left Greencourt so suddenly. That includes Roberta Jones and her family. The Governors stumped up for the trip to France and the truth never came out. As a matter of fact I talked to Roberta on Saturday about Greencourt and it's quite obvious that she hasn't the slightest inkling.'

'She hasn't?' For the first time Max showed some emotion. A delighted smile lit up his bronzed face. 'Nor her parents? Really?'

'Yes, really,' said Miss Gates, drily. 'So all your efforts this term have, in fact, been a complete waste of time. You have showed her rather special consideration, haven't you? Just in case something might click in her memory? And you really had no need to bother.'

'Hey, that's an unkind thing to say!' Max suddenly looked angry.

'Unkind or not,' broke in Miss Welbeck, 'this brings us to the question of the maths exam. We were both very impressed with the mark that Roberta achieved. I'm afraid it will be necessary for us to check through all the papers.'

'There's nothing peculiar about those!' exclaimed Max. 'If that's what you're thinking.'

'We'd like to check them, all the same,' insisted Miss Welbeck. 'Where are they?'

'They're back at the cottage,' said Max sulkily. 'And Katie's out today in the car, so she can't come and fetch me and beside –' he looked at his watch, 'I'm due to take II Alpha in five minutes.'

Miss Welbeck picked up the internal phone and dialled.

'I'll ask Hodkin to drive you to your cottage so that you can pick up the exam papers. It won't take long,' she said pleasantly. 'Before you leave, I suggest you find a prefect to go and sit in on your class for the time being.'

Fifteen minutes later, Max re-entered the Principal's study with II Alpha's maths exam papers rolled up in a bundle under his arm. He plonked them down on Miss Welbeck's leather-topped desk, almost jauntily.

'Here they are. They're all in order.'

He threw himself back in the chair while the two women sorted through the rather dog-eared papers. Miss Gates withdrew two of them and held them up between forefinger and thumb, looking quite shocked.

'Whatever happened to these? They look as though they've been in a washing machine.'

'They blew away into the sea, while I was marking them,' said Max nonchalantly. 'Luckily, I got 'em back and they soon dried out in the sun. The top one's Bobbie's – I mean, Roberta's.'

Miss Gates picked up a pencil and checked through it carefully.

'Hmmmm,' she said at the end. She was a little put out. 'Yes, I make it sixty-one per cent. Very smudged in places, but that's not her fault. Quite a good paper in fact.'

'I'm glad you agree,' said Max. 'The other one's Rebecca Mason's – hopeless.'

'Let me see both papers,' said Miss Welbeck suddenly.

She examined them, holding each one up in turn, looking to where each girl had written her name, at the top of the first page.

'How do you know which is Roberta's and which is Rebecca's?' she asked.

'Well, their names –' began Max.

'But both names are badly smudged!' observed Miss Welbeck. 'I can make out that they both begin with R and are both the same length, but that's all.

And as both girls have very similar handwriting, why are you so sure which is which?'

'Well,' said Max, 'I suppose I just took an inspired guess. If you compare the marks they've had in term, then there's no question –'

'I had the impression that Rebecca had been doing rather better lately,' said Miss Gates. 'I think Pippa –'

'Yes, Pippa Fellowes-Walker has been helping her,' said Max. 'Doing her homework for her too, I expect, so I haven't taken that very seriously.'

'How seriously do you take Roberta's marks through the term then?' inquired Miss Gates. 'Haven't you been giving *her* a great deal of help?'

'I'm sure Bobbie's done much better than twenty-eight per cent!' said Max, quite heatedly. 'I'm sure I've got the papers the right way round!'

'You *wanted* her to do well. You made up your mind in advance that hers was the good paper and Rebecca's was the bad one,' said Miss Welbeck sharply. 'You may be right. You may be wrong. But you didn't even bother to check! This is disgraceful. Worse than Greencourt. A lot depends on it, as it happens. It's quite essential that we find out which paper is which.'

The Principal rose to her feet, her lips set in a hard line.

'Go back to II Alpha and take your maths class, Dennis. Ask Rebecca Mason to come to my study at once and to bring her maths exercise book. Carry on teaching here until Thursday morning, when your contract expires. As far as I'm concerned, that won't be a moment too soon.'

After Max had gone, Miss Gates looked at her watch.

'I have to take a tutorial,' she said.

'Then run along, Evelyn,' said the Principal. 'I'll see to Rebecca. By studying her handwriting carefully, I'll soon be able to establish which paper is hers. I wonder which one it is? I must confess, I am going to find this very interesting.'

THIRTEEN
Term's End

Rebecca didn't hear Max coming back to the form room. She was well into her book. Since Saturday she'd been buoyed up by the feeling that they were doing something to get the charity money back. That buoyant feeling had come to a head early this morning when the six of them had carried the cash box back to school in triumph. But now the excitement was over, a dull heavy ache had settled back inside her. Term was nearly over now. Next term, all the changes would come. Much better to escape into a book than think about unpleasant things. At the moment, the world of Blandings Castle seemed infinitely preferable to real life.

Roberta, on the other hand, heard Max's footsteps at once.

'He's coming!' she whispered to Debbie. 'I'll be summoned to see the Head now! I wonder what they've decided?'

'Let's cross fingers,' said Debbie, as the door opened.

Max stood framed in the doorway, but didn't come in. To Roberta's annoyance he didn't even look at her. He peered round the door and called to Rebecca, sitting at the back of the class.

'Rebecca Mason. Come out here in the corridor – and bring your maths workbook with you.'

Sue gave her a hard nudge.

Guiltily, Rebecca shoved Wodehouse inside her desk, got her exercise book and went out to join Max in the corridor. She couldn't imagine why he'd called her out there.

The senior prefect gathered together some work she'd been doing and waited for Max to come in and take over. But first he hustled Rebecca along the corridor to the top of the stairs, where they couldn't be seen from the form room.

'Miss Welbeck wants you to go straight to her study,' he said, 'and take that book with you.'

He hesitated, as though he wanted to say something else. Rebecca noticed that he looked rather agitated and she waited expectantly.

'Look, Rebecca,' he glanced around, almost furtively. 'There's only a few minutes of the lesson left now. I don't want you to come back here. When you've seen Miss Welbeck I want you to go straight to the library and sit there and wait for me. And you're to tell *no one* about anything, until we've had a talk. Promise me!'

'The library?' Rebecca was amazed. But she nodded. 'All right then.'

What on earth was going on?

When she entered the study and Miss Welbeck showed her the two exam papers, all withered and smudged, Rebecca stared at them in shock.

'Whatever happened to them?' she blurted out.

'An accident,' Miss Welbeck said hastily. 'The point is, Rebecca, the names are smudged. Which one is yours?'

'That one!' said Rebecca promptly, pointing.

'Let's make quite sure, shall we?' said Miss Welbeck, holding out her hand for Rebecca's workbook. She took it and opened it at random, then checked it carefully against the two exam papers on her desk. 'Yes, you are quite right.'

She closed Rebecca's exercise book and handed

it back. She was smiling.

'You achieved sixty-one per cent in the maths exam. Well done.'

'Sixty-one per cent!' gasped Rebecca. 'But–'

'The twenty-eight per cent belongs to Roberta Jones, I'm afraid. There's been a mix-up. These things happen.'

'Then –' A feeling of great joy was welling up inside Rebecca. 'Does that mean I might go up into III Alpha after all – into Court House like the others?'

'Without question,' nodded the Principal. 'Run back to your lesson now. Don't say anything to Roberta Jones, yet. I'll arrange for Miss Gates to break the news to her as soon as possible.'

Break the news! As she left the study, Rebecca wanted to laugh, hysterically. Roberta wasn't exactly going to be upset! But even her happiness wouldn't possibly match Rebecca's at that moment. She was delirious.

She wanted to run back up the stairs, whooping for joy, and rush straight into the form room and whisper the good news to Tish and Sue and Margot and Elf! And then find Mara!

But she steadied herself. The library! She'd

promised Max. She had to get a grip on herself and go and sit quietly in the library and wait for him.

'He wants to apologise!' thought Rebecca as she sat in the big window seat, waiting. She should have felt furious with him, but she didn't. She felt quite light-hearted with happiness. 'He let the sea get on the exam papers! He must have been down on that rock again, when he marked them! Isn't that just typical! Oh, I can't wait to tell Tish and Sue, they'll see the funny side . . .'

She started to smile to herself and she was still smiling when Max walked into the library. One look at her face told him the truth.

'So I *did* get the papers the wrong way round, after all!' he groaned, covering his face with his hands in mock shame and then sitting down next to her. 'Did I?'

'Yes!' said Rebecca happily.

'I want to apologise –' he began.

'No, it's all right!' said Rebecca, starting to get to her feet. She didn't want to listen to Max's apologies. She'd spare him that! She wanted to find her friends – *now*. Before biology started! 'I'm glad it's been sorted out.'

'No, wait.' He grabbed her arm, urgently, and

176

pulled her back down on to the seat. 'Don't go. It's not only that I want to apologise, though I do, of course. It's Roberta.'

Rebecca stared at him in surprise. He seemed very agitated.

'I expect Miss Welbeck's told you that it was me who pinched your charity money and that I got the sack from Greencourt, but –'

Rebecca's head began to spin dizzily. *Max* – the charity money? Greencourt? That was the school that Roberta used to go to! She remembered her happy cry, on the very first morning of term: '*I remember! You were at Greencourt!*' And suddenly Rebecca had a vivid mental picture of Max, his back to the class, chalking up a number then freezing – freezing at Roberta's words! Of course. Why had she never, never suspected anything?

Although Rebecca's face portrayed her astonishment, Max just went rattling on. Gradually his words began to untangle in her brain.

'I soon realised that Bobbie didn't remember any scandal,' he was saying, 'but I could never be sure that something might not stir in her memory, especially if she found she didn't like me. So I set out to pretend that she was my favourite and hoped it would make her like *me* a lot.'

'It did,' said Rebecca. 'And she still does.'

'I realise that. But you needn't look so disgusted. The truth is that she's a good kid, she tries hard.'

He looked Rebecca straight in the eye and she saw that he genuinely felt kindly towards Roberta. Now she knew why he was agitated.

'She'd be so disappointed if she knew all this, wouldn't she?' murmured Rebecca.

'Yes,' said Max. 'I think it would be desperately sad if Bobbie found out about what happened at Greencourt.'

'So do I,' said Rebecca.

'It would make her think everything was a sham,' said Max. 'Which it wasn't. Can you keep it from everybody?'

'I can't keep all this from my two best friends,' said Rebecca. Her mind was feeling rather numb. 'That would be just too much to ask. But – we – the three of us, we'll make sure that Roberta never, ever finds out.'

'You will?' They both stood up. Max looked tremendously relieved. 'And Miss Welbeck or Gatesy wouldn't ever say anything to her, would they?'

'Of course not!' said Rebecca. She wanted to add: *Whatever made you think that they'd told me?* But she didn't.

Roberta had to go and see Miss Gates during the biology lesson and she came back, smiling, just in time for morning break.

'You'll be getting some good news very soon, Rebecca,' she said. 'I've already had mine. I'm going into III Beta after all, because of my maths – so I'll be in Norris House with Debbie and the twins! What's more, you can have my place in Court House and in III Alpha as well.'

Rebecca, Tish and Sue all nodded and smiled and said nothing.

'Of course, Gatesy would never have agreed to it in a million years. It was Max. He knew how much I wanted to be with my friends and so he wangled it somehow. Told them some fantastic story about our marks getting mixed up. D'you think that could possibly be true?'

'Well, I suppose it's possible,' said Rebecca.

'No,' Roberta shook her head. She looked animated, almost pretty. She never ever wore her hair in those lumpy plaits these days. 'I think he did it for me. Well, you as well,' she added hastily.

There was a faraway look in her eyes.

'I can hardly believe that the term's almost over and he'll be going. I'll never forget Max, as long as I live. He really is a very wonderful person.'

'One of the best,' said Tish.

As Debbie came up and bore Roberta away, Rebecca and her two closest friends exchanged looks. Soon, very soon now, Max was just going to be a beautiful memory for Roberta. They would never do anything to spoil it.

Tish and Sue each took Rebecca by the hand.

'Come on, let's find the other three,' said Sue.

'Mara's got a cake –' said Tish. 'It's covered in chocolate icing and little sweets – it's been hidden away in Miss Morgan's office since Saturday morning!'

'Why?' asked Rebecca.

'Her father sent it for an end-of-term celebration. We just didn't know what to do with it. We haven't felt like a celebration, any of us.'

'Until now!' said Sue. She laughed and flicked back a strand of sandy-coloured hair from her forehead. 'We know exactly what to do with it now!'

'You bet!' cried Rebecca in delight – and off they ran.

Term's end was full of goodbyes.

Goodbye to Juniper House and dormitory number six with its primrose-coloured walls and big windows and its view of the sea. Goodbye to Miss Morgan, the junior House Mistress. They would never be juniors again! Goodbye to *The J.J.* which had given them so much fun and plenty of drama, too. Susannah Skelhorn would be its editor next term.

Goodbye to Audrey Maxwell, who had produced a brilliant issue of *The Trebizon Journal* in her last term, with the juniors well represented in it. And to Jacquinda Meredith and Joanne Hissup, who were both going up to Oxford, and all the rest of the Upper Sixth. Goodbye to their form-mistress, Miss Heath, and the funny little II Alpha form room stuck up high in old building.

Rebecca's first year at Trebizon was over.

As well as the goodbyes, she said a special thank-you to Pippa for helping her with her maths.

'In a way, though you don't know it, you've helped *me*,' said Pippa.

'I have?' asked Rebecca in surprise.

Pippa, who would be going into the Upper Sixth next term, had been voted in as next year's editor of

The Trebizon Journal.

'It was neck and neck,' said Pippa, 'and I think the thing that really decided it was the illustrations I did for your essay, 'A Winter's Morning', remember?'

Rebecca was never likely to forget her prize-winning essay in the school magazine the previous term. For her, it had been a high point of the year.

'The drawings were beautiful!' she exclaimed. 'That snowman – and the birds. And the poor little squirrel, frozen in the ice.'

'But it was what you'd written that sparked them off! So you see, Rebecca, I've got something to thank *you* for. I've always wanted to be editor of *The Trebizon* one day.' She looked very happy at that moment. 'I never, ever thought I would be!'

Rebecca wasn't really convinced that she'd had very much to do with it, but she felt a surge of pleasure, all the same.

Then something else happened, on the last morning of term, that brought even greater pleasure – it was so totally unexpected.

'I'm sorry you won't be coming to the County Sports with us this afternoon, Rebecca,' said Miss Willis.

Rebecca was silent, as all the old disappointment

over that returned with a dull thud. Her parents were back home in London now, just back. How different things might have been! They might have been coming down to the west country today, to see her run this afternoon, as Tish's family were.

'But I've got some good news for you on a different front,' continued the blonde games mistress. 'You can count yourself lucky that you were born in this county –'

Rebecca wondered what was coming next. It was true that, by some fluke, Mr Mason had been working in the west country when Rebecca was born, although they'd returned to London when she was three months old.

Suddenly Rebecca realised what *might* be coming next and a thrill of shock ran down her spine. That tall lady who'd been walking round the tennis courts with Miss Willis recently, watching some of them play – the county tennis scout, someone had said!

'That's right, Rebecca,' said Sara Willis, reading her face. 'You've been "spotted" as having special promise. You've been selected for a new county scheme for junior players – indoor training in the winter months. Your parents will be getting a letter, giving all the details.'

'Me?' Rebecca felt dizzy with excitement. 'But I've only just started –' Something else to thank Pippa for!

'It's the promise that counts.' The teacher laughed. 'I can see us losing you from athletics again next summer. But, am I right? I think you prefer tennis.'

'Well –' Rebecca was still feeling rather stunned. She'd never thought about it deeply until this moment. 'Why, yes . . . maybe I do.'

Tish and Sue hugged her when they heard the news. They went for a last exhilarating surf-ride together before they packed. The bay looked at its most glorious. Later, just before dinner, they joined up with the other three and went and had a look at Court House from the outside. It was a lovely, rambling old place covered in Virginia creeper, on the far side of the Hilary.

'And that's where we'll be living for the next three years,' sighed Mara, a peaceful expression on her face.

'They share studies in threes,' said Elf. 'We must bag two right next door to each other.'

'Studies!' said Margot.

They continued to gaze at Court House.

'Not bad, is it?' said Tish.

'Not bad at all!' agreed Rebecca.

After dinner, everything broke up. Max was the first to go. The familiar red sports car drew up in the main forecourt to collect him. He came jauntily down the steps for the last time. A small gaggle of admirers waited to see him off, with Roberta Jones in the forefront.

He gave them all a wave, hesitated, then smiled

across to Roberta – 'Goodbye, Bobbie!' – before climbing into the car.

Roberta waved and waved until the car was out of sight and then linked arms with Debbie Rickard.

Upstairs, in the panelled study, Miss Welbeck and Miss Gates had been standing by the window and had watched his departure.

'I made a mistake with that young man,' murmured the Principal.

'He was a dead loss,' said Miss Gates.

Miss Welbeck gazed out through the window at Roberta Jones and Debbie Rickard, walking arm in arm, past the big cedar tree which was an oasis of dappled shade in the strong July sunlight. Their heads were close together and Debbie, no doubt, was comforting Roberta.

'No, Evelyn,' she said at last, with the merest hint of a smile. 'His presence here was not all loss. Not entirely.'

Even Rebecca would have agreed with that.

Boy Trouble at TREBIZON

Read about
Rebecca's
next term
at **TREBIZON**
in this special
extract . . .

ONE
Rebecca's Ambition

'I'm not interested in boys,' said Rebecca Mason before they went back to school. She was bouncing a ball up and down on her racket. 'I'm going to stick to tennis. You won't catch me going to those dances and things and mixing with the boys from Garth College.'

'Nor me,' said Ishbel Anderson, who was called Tish for short. 'It's bad enough having a brother there.'

As juniors at Trebizon, a boarding school in the west country, they had led a fairly sheltered existence. But this term Rebecca and her friends were going up into the Middle School – and would be allowed more social life. Garth College was a boys' boarding school nearby and a lot of the Trebizon girls had brothers there. (Robbie Anderson went there and so did Sue Murdoch's two brothers, David and Edward.) A certain amount of intermingling went on at weekends, but that prospect didn't interest Rebecca very much.

Tennis was her big interest in life these days . . . for a good reason!

Her home was in south London but she'd actually been born in the west country – in the same county as Trebizon itself. This accident of birth qualified her for a new county scheme for junior players. Last term while she'd been playing tennis at school she had been spotted by Mrs Seabrook (the county tennis scout down there) and picked for the junior reserve squad, a group of eight boys and girls who were to have special training through the winter months. The very best of them might get promoted to the County Junior D squad at Christmas.

For the summer holidays, Mrs Seabrook had arranged for Rebecca to join a tennis club near her London home. *She has a natural talent for the game and great speed around the court*, she had written to Mr and Mrs Mason, *but she is entering tennis late and has a lot of ground to make up*. Rebecca had played at the club almost every day and taken tennis lessons as well. She also practised her strokes for hours on end against the high brick wall at the back of their London house. She was making progress at an unprecedented rate.

But there was something on her mind, as Tish discovered when she rang her up towards the end of the summer holidays and invited her to stay.

'Oh, Tish, I'd love to come to your house! I've never been! But –'

'But what?'

'It's my tennis. They've put me into the Trebizon Open Tournament next Sunday. Mum and Dad are driving me back to school two days early, because Mrs Seabrook thinks I should be in it.'

'You must be getting good!' exclaimed Tish. 'Robbie goes in for that. Hey!' She suddenly realised something. 'If you're going back early you can get two really good rooms in Court House, before anyone arrives! One for us three, you and me and Sue, and one for –'

'– the other three. Margot and Mara and Elf!' Rebecca smiled down the phone. 'I'd already thought of that!'

'Anyway, what's the problem?' Tish asked.

'That's not till next weekend, so what's to stop you coming here for a few days first?'

'The problem is my tennis. It's awful. And guess who my partner's going to be in the tournament?'

'Superman?'

'Shut up, Tish!' laughed Rebecca. 'It's nearly as bad. Someone called David Driscoll. He's part of the county tennis set-up. He's the man who's going to be teaching our group! I'm dreading it . . .'

'Well, why not come here and dread it in comfort?' Tish inquired.

'I dunno, Tish . . .' Rebecca felt torn. 'I'd *so* like to come. But I daren't stop practising. I've joined this club, you see, and we've got this big wall at the back of the house –'

'But we've got our own tennis court!' exclaimed Tish, now that she understood. 'Didn't I ever tell you?'

'No!' Rebecca was amazed.

'And Robbie can coach you!'

'Robbie – your brother?'

'Yes. He's really good – he wins all the tennis cups at Garth. He's working on a farm in the afternoons but he's here in the mornings. He'll help you. Say you'll come! Ask your parents – ring back!'

'You bet!' said Rebecca.

That conversation had taken place on Sunday.

Now it was Tuesday morning. Rebecca was standing outside the gate of the Andersons' hard tennis court, discussing school with Tish while waiting for her first tennis lesson with Robbie.

She could see him in the distance, rear view only, slim hips and long legs clad in old denim trousers. His head was under the bonnet of an elderly black saloon parked round the back of the house. Helen, Tish's elder sister, was standing beside him. He'd said he would only be a moment – but it was turning out to be a very long one.

'Oh dear,' said Tish. 'Helen's asked him to fix her car before she drives back to London. He'll be hours. He's crazy about cars – he can't wait for the day when he'll be old enough to have a licence.'

'Oh,' said Rebecca.

In the distance, the engine gave a sudden loud roar. Robbie slammed down the bonnet, spoke quickly to Helen and then ran and jumped into the driving seat.

'Helen's letting him drive it!' exclaimed Tish. 'Oh, she's stupid. She always lets him get round her.'

Sure enough the car reversed, then turned, then mounted the expanse of bumpy rough grass that lay between the back of the house and the tennis court. The next moment it was bumping and jolting slowly over the tussocks towards them.

'But he's not old enough to have a licence!' said Rebecca, alarmed.

'He doesn't need one, as long as he stays in our grounds,' said Tish. 'He's been practising since he was thirteen. Nobody's car's safe when Robbie's around!'

'Is he going to run us over?'

'Shouldn't think so!' grinned Tish.

Robbie braked hard alongside them and wound the window down. His black curly hair stood on end, there was a smear of oil on his forehead and he was smiling happily.

'Sorry, Rebecca!' he shouted above the engine noise. 'Just got to get a bit of driving in before Helen goes. Won't be long. You two have a knock-up!'

He revved up the engine and then the car went lurching off around the outside of the tennis court and through an open gate that led into the paddock beyond, honking loudly. Half a dozen young ewes,

Dr Anderson's pride and joy, at once stopped their peaceful grazing, picked up their short little legs and wobbled away as fast as they could go, all in a huddle, baaa-ing crossly, until they reached the hedge in the far corner of the paddock. They then resumed their grazing beneath a spreading oak tree, a safe and secluded spot.

'Lunatic!' said Tish. 'Come on, let's play.'

They opened the gate of the tennis court and went inside, wound the net up to its correct height and then started to knock the ball backwards and forwards. Rebecca thought that the sound of the ball thwacking against racket strings was one of the nicest sounds on earth and she began to feel very happy.

'Rebeck!' exclaimed Tish, racing to retrieve a forehand and only just getting it back. 'Wow! What's happened to you?'

Rebecca was already up at the net and put Tish's loose return away with an angled backhand volley. She couldn't help laughing at the expression on Tish's face. Tish was a very sound player and even three months ago could have beaten Rebecca easily. Now she was flabbergasted.

'Have I improved?'

'Improved. It's amazing!'

They settled down to a hard knock-up, pelting the balls backwards and forwards. Out of the corner of her eye, Rebecca could see across the hedge and into the paddock. The battered old black car roared round and round the field, bucking and roaring over the bumpy patches. Each time the car came close to the hedge she could glimpse Robbie, hunched over the steering wheel, the breeze from the window blowing his hair around, a look of glazed ecstasy on his face. Then with a great deal of brrrmphing and revving and gear changing, he would take the car into a tight U-turn and *brrroooommmmm* off across the field again.

'Does he ever hit anything?' she called out to Tish.

'Not very often!' replied Tish, sending up a high lob.

A moment later there came a screech of brakes and a tremendous juddering sound as Robbie, coming up to the hedge and turning too late, had to stop dead.

'Oh, no!' said Tish.

The car slid forward, before Robbie could stop it, and gently nose-dived into the wide ditch that ran beneath the hedge.

Glancing back towards the house, Rebecca caught a glimpse of Helen's pale face at an upstairs window. She seemed to be waving her arms.

Robbie switched off the engine and climbed out of the car, shouting through the hedge in the direction of the tennis court.

'Quick, you two, come and help!'

Rebecca and Tish ran round into the paddock and tried hard not to laugh at the sight of the car, its front wheels hanging down in the ditch. No damage had been done.

'Come on, help me push it out before Helen sees!' said Robbie, already down in the ditch and getting his shoulder under the front bumper. 'She gets excited.'

'She has seen,' Tish stated calmly. 'And she may be excited already.'

Luckily Robbie was tall and strong. With the three of them heaving and lifting and puffing, they had the car safely out of the ditch by the time Helen arrived. She was smartly dressed and wearing high-heeled shoes, ready to drive back to her flat in London.

'Is everything all right?' she asked suspiciously.

'Fine!' said Robbie nonchalantly, though his face was still red from his exertions. 'I've given it a good run and the timing's okay. It was just the plugs. They were filthy.'

'I don't see why you have to drive it so fast,' said Helen. 'I think I'd better take it now.'

'Okay.' Robbie looked disappointed. 'Let me just put it back on the drive for you.' He jumped into the driving seat quickly, before Helen could refuse, and held open the passenger door for her. They reversed and then went slowly and very soberly off through the paddock gate. Rebecca and Tish walked along behind.

They watched as Robbie parked the car on the back drive. While Helen went into the house to get her overnight bag, he got out a handkerchief and polished the windscreen for her, although it was already perfectly clean.

'Robbie!' yelled Tish, cupping her hands to her mouth. 'Rebecca's waiting!'

Robbie shoved the handkerchief in his pocket, surveyed the car once more and then tore himself away.

'Coming!' he shouted. 'Got my racket there?'

As Robbie ambled slowly and dreamily across

the grass towards them, every so often glancing back at the car as though he were saying goodbye to it, Tish whispered to Rebecca:

'Some car or other will get Robbie into a whole lot of trouble one day!'